Ruthie—
Good luck in the next part of your story. Enjoy each chapter, they go so fast! ♡

Unparalleled

By Whitney Ivey

© 2022 Whitney Ivey. All rights reserved.

ISBN: 979-8-9865371-0-8

All rights reserved. This book, or parts thereof, may not be reproduced in any form, stored in any retrieval system, or transmitted in any form by any means – electronic, mechanical, photocopy, recording, or otherwise – without permission of the author, except provided by the United States of America copyright law or in the case of brief quotations embodied in critical articles and reviews.

Editor: Sharp Editorial

Dedication

To my #IveyLeague:

Jebby –
Since 2003, you've continued to give me a love that is so unparalleled, it created a new universe. It's everything. It's just *that*. I am forever the luckiest woman to walk this Earth. "If you live to be 100, I want to live to be 100, minus one day, so I never have to live a day without you."
– Winnie the Pooh.
I love you, infinitely.

Big, BayBay, and Jelly –
I hope you are proud, and I hope this shows that there is *nothing* in this world you can't do if you want it.
You are forever my greatest accomplishments.
Be kind. Make the right choices.
And be the best version of yourselves you can be.

Love, Ludge, Luyu.

Acknowledgments

To Laci & the Sharp Editorial Team: Thank you for your advice, collaboration, and support throughout this process. Without it, this book is just an idea that never makes it onto a page. You're the real MVP. I am forever grateful to you.

To my husband, Jeb: Thank you for being my inspiration, my sounding board, and my number one fan. This story has no life without you. Thank you for bringing me along to see the world—watching you play remains my favorite thing to do, ever. I am so proud of us. No marriage is without work, but anything working toward you is easy.

To Jaxon, Bayland, and Marli Joe: Thank you for making me a mom; it is truly my greatest joy.

To my family: Mommy & Daddy: Thank you for instilling so much confidence in me that writing a book seemed like just a thing. You're the greatest parents that ever existed. You are my first example of true and unconditional love, and because of that, when I found Jebby, I knew instantly.

Courtney, Derek, & Ashley: Thank you for having my back always. Sibling love is difficult at times, but my life would be void without it. I love you.

Poppy: Thank you for pushing me to take a chance with *him,* in only the way you could. I wish he could have met you. I miss you.

To our grandparents, Nanny, Poppy (RIP), Grandma Claire (RIP), Grandpa Al (RIP), GG, Moore (RIP), Papa Aldo (RIP), & Noni (RIP): Thank you for paving the way and making all this possible.

To my nieces and nephews: Thank you for letting me have auntie love. It started with my Madipants, and I am so lucky it keeps going. I am here for you all, always.

To my entire in-law family: Thank you for accepting me as yours from day one. To say I lucked out with all of you is an understatement. I have never felt out of place, as a part of your family. I love you all.

To my forever friends, Jeni, Jessi, JoJo, Kimi, Kira, Yaz, Dyani, D, Hada, Mervi, Celine, Sugar Bear, & Ali Qat: I have a small and mighty circle and dare I say without it I'd be a shell of myself. Thank you for always answering, thank you for always picking up where we leave off, and thank you for your everlasting love and friendships. I ludge and love you all to the ends of the Earth.

To Noel (RIP) and Mitch: Thank you for giving me, Jebby, he is everything to me.

To PapaJoe (RIP): Thank you for your immense hand in raising the greatest human I know. It is hard to see a future without you in it, but we have constant reminders of you, in your children and grandchildren. You will be forever missed and imbedded in our hearts.

To our friends in Iceland, Finland, France, & Germany: Thank you for being our home away from home for 16 years. We miss you all.

Table of Contents

Prologue 1

Chapter One 2

Chapter Two 13

Chapter Three 24

Chapter Four 35

Chapter Five 55

Chapter Six 88

Chapter Seven 123

Chapter Eight 131

Chapter Nine 139

Chapter Ten 146

Chapter Eleven 160

Chapter Twelve 170

Chapter Thirteen 178

Chapter Fourteen 192

Epilogue 205

Prologue

"But Daddy, he's my best friend. How can I not tell him?"

"Because baby girl, that's how it works. You knew that from the beginning. That's why you were given a choice. We were all given a choice."

"But I didn't know it would be like this."

"I know. But would you have chosen differently had you understood the meaning back then?" he asked.

"No," I replied with certainty.

The absolute truth is that I wouldn't have chosen differently. Regardless of how hard this would be for the both of us, I wouldn't trade him for anything in my world or his.

Only one thing would make it possible for me to see him again, and even then, it wasn't a guarantee because I would have no memory of him at all.

But none of that mattered because he did not see me the way I saw him. For the last two years, after realizing exactly how I felt, the only thing I wanted was for him to see me, really see me. But he didn't, and in two weeks, it won't matter. He will never be given a chance to figure it out. It's against the rules for me to tell him, so we will just be lost without each other.

I will be lost until I find him again.

If I find him again.

Chapter One
(Derek)

I was three years old when I remember meeting Essi for the first time. Although we may have played together before that, my memory only starts in pieces around the age of three.

She was my best friend. We were inseparable for close to 13 years. We didn't care how weird it was to have a best friend of the opposite sex, but then again, who really cares about that when you're three? I didn't have many other friends growing up because I loved being around Essi so much. Other kids teased me about it, but it didn't matter. If I could have had her as my one friend for the rest of my life, I would have been truly okay with that.

We knew we had a special bond from the beginning, and I don't mean because it was "love at first sight." Not at age three, anyway. Although now I can look back and be certain that I loved her from the very start.

I think our special bond stemmed from the fact that we were the only ones who could see each other.

Ha. I know what you're thinking, but no, I'm not crazy.

Yes, Essi was my "imaginary" friend, but she was anything but imaginary.

Now you can understand why this affected my friendships with other kids, even why my parents had me seeing a therapist at age eight.

Who does that? Aren't parents supposed to support their children's imaginations?

Looking back, I guess it was a little odd that Essi was still "around" when I entered my teen years, but at the time, it couldn't have been more normal, at least to us anyway.

Essi was nothing short of amazing. I told her that often when we were older, and she always accused me of making fun of her height. She was playful like that. She was funny, loving, and loyal, and she taught me everything about being a good friend. She had the bluest eyes and hair that somehow changed from the perfect honey-blond when she was little to an even more perfect chocolate brown as we got older. I always thought that contrast was unique, but it could have just been her that I was fond of. Essi was tiny, too, a whopping five feet two inches tall, and she was as feisty as they come. I loved that about her. I didn't care what anyone thought, but I guess that's easy when no one else could hear what you have to say. Not in my world, at least.

And she was beautiful.

My god, she was beautiful.

I miss her laugh. It was one of those laughs that you are almost embarrassed when it comes out because it's so loud that you think everyone is staring, but then you can't help but join in because it's contagious. I would actually turn red in the face when she started, and then we would laugh hysterically because I was embarrassed.

Of what?

Other people hearing her?

That concept always eluded me, but we got a good laugh out of it all the time. Essi would laugh so hard that she would end up in tears on a regular basis. Her laugh was unusual. And the crazier part is that after all this time when I close my eyes, I can still see her face and hear her laugh as clear as day. I stopped dead in my tracks on campus today because I could have sworn I heard it again. It put me in a daze.

She was what we consider an imaginary friend, but she was not made from my imagination. My mind did not muster her up to help me cope with something traumatic. I did not bring her to life to feel accepted by someone else. She was as real as the air I breathe and the ground I walk on, and I miss her every day.

In Essi's world, the equivalent of an imaginary friend was called a "link," a link from the Parallel to Earth. However, for them, links were a normal part of everyday life, the exact opposite for us on Earth.

Most kids lose their imaginary friends at some point in their early childhood, and few get to keep them around after that. I was lucky enough to be one of those few. I'd like to say it's because children's minds are developing. In fact, I should know that to be true. According to all my studies, to someday become a psychiatrist, I'm supposed to believe this, but no amount of schooling or practice in that profession could sway my opinion of her.

Essi and I were inseparable until the day I turned 16. We did absolutely everything together. She was even my date to my first high school dance. Although my actual date didn't know that.

That was the last day I ever saw her.

I still remember how I felt when I was around her, how she *made* me feel. It was like nothing else I've ever experienced.

Essi was there for me through everything in my childhood and into my teens—the good, the bad, and most importantly, the day my dad died, quite possibly the worst day of my life.

There just wasn't another person on the planet that knew me like she did. And at 11:59 pm, one minute before my 16th birthday, when I saw Essi for the last time, it wasn't because my mind had developed, and I no longer needed her or that I made a choice to let her go. It was because she had to leave. We had to say goodbye because of the rules in the Parallel.

Although we knew that day would come, we thought about everything we could do to try to change it. For years, we dreaded that day, but that's just how it was for them. As a part of the Parallel's rules, links were broken at 16, no matter what.

Of course, friendships ended before those dates, too. Some people moved on because they were convinced (by their parents, usually) that what they were seeing wasn't real, or they found other friends and didn't need the imaginary ones anymore. Neither was the case for us. Essi and I held on until the very end.

There was a system in place that kept them safe and their world hidden. It seemed ruthless, but when I turned 16, Essi had to leave, and the door to our worlds shut forever. Essi never really talked much about the rules, but I remember wishing we could be the first to break them. When she left me that night, my heart broke for the second time in my life.

The majority of imaginary friends disappeared way before Essi. Most children are told repeatedly that their link is not real. It's hard to keep someone around when no one else can see them, and all your "real" friends won't talk to you because they think you're weird. The way Essi explained it, was the less energy you give them, the harder it is for their door to open and come back, and eventually, it closes for good.

The worst part is the pity you see from other adults like they're saying to you with their eyes, "You poor thing. You still don't know she's not real."

I hated that.

And, of course, it's adorable when you are really little. People even pretend to engage with your imaginary friends when you're that young. When I was four and five, my parents used to have me ask Essi questions in front of their friends, and when I would relay her answer, they would all laugh hysterically and tell me I was cute. That went on for a few years. At first, Essi and I thought it was fun. We even thought it might be a good way to show people she was real, but as we got older, we realized they were doing it to make fun of me. That really pissed off Essi.

All the fun came to a screeching halt when she gave them an answer they didn't think was funny. My mom's friend, Mrs. Cotter, said to me, "Derek, if Essi can go anywhere without being seen, ask her what color my underwear is today." Everyone laughed and encouraged what they thought would be a silly answer, but when I asked Essi and gave them her reply, I was grounded for two weeks.

"Essi says she doesn't know, but maybe Mr. Thomas does."

There was absolute silence, and nobody was laughing anymore. Mr. Cotter stormed out, Mrs. Cotter followed, and I was ordered to my room.

Mr. Thomas was one of our neighbors. Apparently, they spent quite a bit of time together when Mrs. Cotters' husband wasn't home. I didn't know what that meant back then, but Essi was way more mature than me, so she knew what she was doing when she said it. All I did was repeat her answer, yet somehow, I became the creepy kid spying on Mrs. Cotter.

In hindsight, I should have filtered her response a little better, but at the time, they were insinuating that our friendship wasn't real, and we would have tried anything to prove otherwise. It wasn't fair, though. We got in trouble for playing *their* stupid little game.

I'll tell you one thing—I quickly learned to keep her little secrets to myself.

She had a lot of them.

Essi felt so bad that she stayed with me throughout the whole two weeks of my punishment. Of course, minus the time she had to be at home or school. She would curl up in my yellow chair and just sit there. She apologized a thousand times, but it didn't matter because the damage had been done.

Then, it had started—my parents were trying to talk me out of my best friend and her existence.

Once a week, I was sent to a psychiatrist to see if a doctor could "help me." Essi had warned me that they would start to do this. She said it was part of the cycle, and she had rarely heard of situations where it was different, but I always thought I could convince my parents otherwise. I epically failed every time though.

I saw Dr. Lawson once a week for almost two years, but it would have taken a lot more than Dr. Lawson to convince me that Essi did not exist. The doc thought I was making considerable progress over those two years and even suggested I stop going to her for a while to see if I could transition without her. For obvious reasons, I needed her to believe I was making progress.

Essi and I had come up with a plan about a year into my therapy sessions. We decided that everyone would continue to try and "help" me unless I started to pretend and act like Essi wasn't there anymore. At first, Dr. Lawson said she knew what I was doing, but after playing that part for a few months, I think she started to believe I was getting "better." She believed that Essi was showing up less and less throughout my day and eventually was non-existent.

Of course, that was far from the case. There were times Essi would stand behind Dr. Lawson and make faces or move things out of place and wait for Dr. Lawson to start looking for them. I had to do everything in my power to keep a straight face and not burst into laughter, and that was not an easy feat around Essi. She had quite a sense of humor, and we loved to laugh together.

It was so hard not to smile around her.

I'm pretty sure my parents bought into the whole idea that I believed Essi wasn't real, or at least they wanted to, so they ignored what Dr. Lawson called "red flags."

I honestly think I had them fooled until I was about 12 when they caught me painting my room bright green, and without thinking about it, I blamed it on Essi. Green was her favorite color.

At that moment, I saw what I believed to be a mixture of sadness and relief on their faces—sadness because they weren't sure if I was normal, and relief because I was still young enough and not taking life so seriously. I think parents live vicariously through their kids, and if it weren't considered irresponsible, they would act like children more often.

In any case, Mom left the room in tears, and my dad came in and closed the door. He started to talk, and I could hear a little sarcasm in his voice. I knew he was about to make some sort of joke because he used my nickname, and he rarely used that if it wasn't in a playful manner. At least I knew our conversation would be light-hearted. That was a relief.

"D-Man, you and Essi are going to be the death of your mother. You know that, right?" Then, he chuckled a little and asked, "In all seriousness, are you okay, pal?" He paused for a few seconds, but I didn't respond because I knew he wasn't finished. Something profound always came out of my dad's mouth when he asked me if I was okay.

"Your mother and I love you more than anything, and we just need to know you're okay. Listen, I've never told your mother this, and I will deny it to my grave if you ever rat me out, but I can sort of remember having an imaginary friend, too."

I looked at him, puzzled.

"I know," he chuckled and continued. "I don't remember much of him, don't even remember his name, but I still have a few faint memories when I recall being with him—at random places too, but mostly when my parents took me to the beach. We'd always play in the sand. I couldn't tell you why I stopped believing he existed. Maybe I grew up, or I was scared that he wasn't actually real, and I wanted to be normal. Or maybe he just wasn't there anymore. I don't know. The point is, I wish I hadn't stopped having that kind of imagination. It can do wonderful things for you, kiddo, and if I never give you another piece of advice again, listen to me now—hold on to the things that are important to you, and don't ever let someone else take them away." And with another slight chuckle, he said, "Not even your mother, although I know that's easier said than done. You hear me, D-Man?"

I smiled and said, "Thanks, Dad, I hear you." I couldn't get much else out of my mouth through the catch in my throat, but I know he knew that meant more to me than anything else he ever said.

He started for the door, but before he left, he took us both by surprise and addressed Essi for the very first time in my life.

"Essi, if you're really there, and I believe you are, thanks for being such a great friend to my boy. Thanks for keeping him out of trouble… for the most part. You two have a special thing, and something this extraordinary deserves my respect."

He gave a little nod and closed the door behind him as he left.

We were both speechless, which didn't happen very often. I remember how special that moment was for us, and then I remember how quickly it was overturned when my mom bombarded him with questions as he left my room. "What did he say? What's his excuse?" I could hear her loudly whisper, clearly her intention. Her voice and constant inquiries faded into the background as my dad escorted her into their room. I don't know what my dad said to her that day, but my mom never questioned Essi's authenticity again. In fact, she just stopped talking about her altogether. Out of sight, out of mind, I guess, for a couple of years anyway.

Chapter Two
(Derek)

It wasn't more than a few months later that I got the worst news of my life. My dad had been killed in a car accident.

I was walking home from the park a couple of blocks from my house. That had become a normal part of my routine since deciding to give basketball a try—something my dad had been slowly convincing me to do for years. Dad was supposed to meet me there that day to practice my free throws. I was finally going to try out for the basketball team, and he was so excited that he had been meeting me there three days a week for a couple of months. He did his best to teach me the fundamentals and guide me into the type of player I'd become. We had been working on my endurance and my shot, but mostly, we were spending a lot of quality time together, and I loved that.

That day, he didn't show, which wasn't like him, but I knew he would have a good explanation, so I worked on some stuff on my own and then headed home.

Essi met me on my walk, and I could see on her face that something was wrong. She just took my hand and walked beside me but didn't say a word.

Oh, God.

As I got closer to my house, I could see a few cars I didn't recognize, and I didn't think much of it until I saw my mom on the floor in the front doorway. She was sitting with her back against the door frame, her elbows on her knees, and her face was buried in her hands. If you had known to look for it, you could have seen her tears dripping through her fingers from a mile away.

The man kneeling next to her was a sheriff from the Portland Police Department, and I knew in an instant that could only mean one thing.

I let go of Essi's hand and started to run to my house. As I reached the grass, I yelled, "Mom!" and asked the most painfully obvious question, "Where's Dad?"

She stood, and with the most sorrow-filled tone, tilted her head and said, "He loved you so much, Derek."

All I could say was no, over and over. I was hysterical. Mom hugged me tightly, and I just kept asking, "Where is he, Mom? He was supposed to meet me. Where is he?"

I didn't know what else to say.

Loved?

What does that mean?

That's past tense.

That means no longer.

That was not what a 13-year-old boy is supposed to hear about his father.

Loved?

Not me.

Not Dad.

I couldn't make any sense of it. I kept going through his day, wishing I could have changed something. I kept wondering if he hadn't been coming to meet me at the park, would he still be alive?

Is this my fault?

What if I hadn't decided to try out for basketball?

Would that have made a difference?

Of course, those were normal questions for someone in my state of grief, but they put me further into depression. I was genuinely a happy kid, but for the first time, I felt true sadness. I was broken, and so was my heart.

I stayed in my room for weeks. I only came out to eat and shower. I didn't go to school, and the assignments sent home from my teachers started to pile up. I shut everyone out, including Essi. Initially, Mom tried to talk to me a lot, tried to comfort me, but when I kept refusing, she would just go into her room and cry. Truthfully, I think she was looking for comfort from me as well. I could hear her sobbing in the middle of the night, and even though my heart ached for her, I didn't know what to say or do. So, I did and said nothing.

I knew I missed him, but I could never understand my mother's state of turmoil… until Essi left. And that's not even a fair comparison. My mom and dad had been together for 25 years, married for 20. They were high school sweethearts and loved each other intensely. They had the kind of love that makes you believe in love. And then… nothing. He was just gone, and she was alone.

My mom didn't have anyone anymore. My aunt went back home, and my uncle, who lived close, was so sad about my dad that he didn't want to come over because we were too much of a reminder for him.

At least I had Essi. That was a common thought for me throughout my childhood.

I don't need them. I have Essi.

Even though I tried to shut her out, Essi didn't take "no" very well. She didn't talk much during that time, mostly just sat with me in her favorite yellow chair and made sure I was fully stocked on Dr Pepper—the true way to my heart. But she encouraged me to talk to my mom. I should have listened to her. I wish I had shown my mom more compassion and grace during that time, at least shown her that she wasn't alone. To me, though, I lost my dad. I didn't know what it felt like to lose the love of your life.

I would, though.

Eventually, I talked to Mom, and we cried in each other's arms for what felt like days. Our grief was simple, and it was sad, but crying was the best thing for both of us.

When Dad died, the people around me were so worried because I didn't talk to anyone, but most of them didn't know I had Essi. When I said she was there for me through everything, I meant everything. She knew what to say, how to act, when to be silent, and when to completely take my mind off the fact that my dad wasn't here anymore. She was just there, exactly what I needed, and exactly the kind of thing that made me love her more. Sometimes, I think she knew that my dad was going to pass away soon. I don't know why but when I think about it, leading up to that day, she was oddly pushing me to spend more time with him. Maybe it was because he had accepted her into my life, whatever form she came in, and she was fond of that, or maybe she had some weird sense for things like that. I'm not sure, and I never asked.

I didn't want to know the answer.

A few months after his death, things were starting to become more normal around the house. Our routine had picked up again. I finally caught up on all my missed schoolwork, with enormous help from my mom, and there was a sense of peace around us. Mom and I had both accepted the loss of my dad, and even though it was hard, we knew that life was continuing around us, and we had no choice but to join again. We didn't talk much about him, but I know we both thought about him a lot. Sometimes I would catch my mom in a daze, and she would smile. I never interrupted her or questioned what it was she was smiling about because I would catch myself joining in on her memory. I let her have those moments, though. They were few and far between. I could always tell when she recalled something special about my dad. She would have the same look on her face that she did when he was here—complete adoration. Those moments helped her heal, and to be honest, they helped me, too. Once I knew Mom was going to be okay, I realized it was alright for me to let go of the pain as well.

Although thinking about my dad felt heavy, it was always easy to do. There were many reminders around us, which were painful and uplifting at the same time. The house I grew up in would never be the same without him but having his memory and energy all around us was comforting. I was lucky to have pieces of him no matter where I went, but the one piece I felt most grateful to have after he passed was my key.

Just before my dad passed away, he had a small key made for me. He called it my key to life and said that no matter how old I got or wise I would become, there would always be new keys to learn, and that was something he wanted me to remember. On the key was inscribed *"Only he who can see the invisible can do the impossible." – Frank L Gaines*

I was speechless.

He had that effect on me.

He gets me.

"If you're ever in a bad spot, and you need a reminder of the person you are, you can always look at this and know I think you're incredible, and I am blown away by your determination and loyalty. You see the invisible, so I know you will do the impossible, pal."

Tears were filling in my eyes.

"Three rules to stick by in life," he had said. "One, be kind. Two, make the right choice. Sometimes it's the harder one, but you'll know. And number three, be the best Derek you can be. It's not easy being different, but I promise it's worth it."

"Thanks, Dad," I had said as I stared at my key with tears dripping from the tip of my nose directly onto its gold silhouette.

He pulled me from thought and had one more dose of wisdom before leaving my room, perhaps the most important one.

"Oh, and one more thing, sort of an unspoken fourth rule. If she orders the filet, she could very well be the one. A great and strong woman always considers the filet."

I gave him a small smile, and he closed the door.

I recall that conversation like it happened yesterday, and my key to life took its place on the gold chain around my neck and has never left. The rules have stuck with me throughout, and I've made decisions about girls according to his fourth rule. It turns out that the "filet rule" has helped me in numerous ways.

My true keys in life have been my dad, my mom, and Essi, so the necklace has served as a daily reminder that they are always with me.

After Dad passed, I wasn't sure I wanted to play basketball again. I guess you could say I sort of blamed it for the accident, but deep down, I knew he would have wanted me to try, so I started to practice again in hopes of making the summer basketball team. There was still a lot of room for improvement, so I didn't have my hopes up.

I didn't make it.

After that, a couple of kids who had already been playing for a few years had started coming around, asking if I wanted to come out and play at the outdoor courts. At first, I think they asked because they felt bad, not only because they knew about my dad but because I was cut from the summer team. Eventually, I think they asked because they genuinely liked me. I knew it couldn't hurt to go, and it was probably wise to start making other friends as I was getting closer to high school. As much as I loved Essi, and she knew that, I didn't want to be "that" guy. I knew Essi would accept me no matter what, but kids at that age are not as forgiving. First and second impressions were big, and I thought it better to enter high school with a few close friends rather than one best friend no one else could see.

I tried out again that fall, even though I knew I would probably be cut again. It was more as a tribute to my dad. He would have told me to keep trying.

The last few months of his life were quite special for us. We were finally enjoying sports together, and I know he loved that, as I had shown no interest before. Looking back, he just wanted something that could be ours.

My dad was heavily into sports, especially baseball, but once I chose basketball, he didn't care. He most certainly wasn't going to discourage my choice of sport just because it wasn't his favorite. He said, "Basketball will easily become my favorite sport. As long as I'm watching you, that's okay with me, kiddo."

He was so good about that. He let me choose what I was interested in. He and Mom both. They never forced me into anything. They just encouraged me to be involved in something other than Essi, which was funny because no matter what I was doing, she was always there. I had definitely gone through my phases, though. I liked the piano, learned to play the guitar (not very well), and even went to a summer art camp, which, of course, Essi had joined. We caused a lot of trouble that summer. Mom and Dad didn't care what I did, though. They just liked when I wanted to try something new. However, I remember always seeing a little disappointment on my dad's face with my refusal to play any sports. He would casually bring them up, and I would quickly turn them down. He tried his hardest not to show disappointment, but I could see it in his body language. Maybe that's why I wanted to try out for the team; I didn't want to disappoint him again. The way his face lit up when I told him of my interest in basketball was like a kid in a candy store. He was beaming, and he didn't care if I would be the worst basketball player on Earth. He was just excited to be a part of it. Even if he couldn't be a part of it physically, I knew he would be there every step of the way in spirit. And with my history of non-beings, I wasn't going to rule out that he was with me somehow, probably in the front row, beaming with pride.

The thought of that still makes me smile.

He would have been pleasantly surprised when I made the first cut and eventually was asked to be a part of the team. When my coach told me I had been chosen, I walked away smiling, and I looked up and said, "Thanks, Dad."

I know he heard me.

Chapter Three
(Derek)

If I had ever felt a sense of accomplishment like that, I cannot remember it for the life of me. There was nothing like hitting the game-winning shot and having my whole team huddle around me, pat me on the back, and rub my head with pride and gratitude.

That day would have been perfect if I had looked in the stands and seen Essi and my dad in the crowd. For obvious reasons, I didn't see my dad, but I was hopeful that Essi would have shown, even though she was mad at me. But she didn't.

Since making the team, I had spent more time around my teammates and less with her. It wasn't on purpose, though. I hadn't intentionally left her behind, so to speak. I had grown to love playing basketball, and after spending so much time in the gym with the other guys, I had grown fond of them as well.

Of course, I was overly fond of Essi, but this was the first time in my life that I didn't feel safe telling my new friends about my lifelong imaginary one. They wouldn't have understood, and Essi couldn't wrap her head around the fact that I cared.

"What happens in two years?" I asked Essi. She just stared at me with her arms crossed and nothing to say. "What happens in one year, nine months and four days, to be exact, when *you* have to leave?"

The emphasis on the word "you" wasn't fair. Even though she was the one leaving me, it was a bad choice of words, and I wished I could have taken it back as soon as I said it. I could see in her eyes how hurtful that was, but I had to try to get her to understand that when she leaves me, I would be left with no one.

I'm making it worse.

"Ess," I said with a disappointing sigh, "If I don't start to create friendships with other real kids, and then you leave, I'll be here with no one. I can't handle that."

There wasn't anything about that sentence or question that Essi heard besides the word "real."

So much worse.

Shit.

I regretted using it immediately. If Essi was anything, she was real, and although I did not intend for my thoughts to come out like that, the path to hell was paved with good intentions.

It didn't matter, though. That hit home for her. She didn't care that she was not real to anyone else, but she cared that she was real to me. I could tell she was finished with our conversation.

She turned her back to me, and without a word, she walked away.

"Ess," I called out after her. "Essi, come back! Please! I didn't mean it like that!"

She put up her hand as she walked away from me, and I knew that nothing I could say at that moment would make it better. For the first time, I had made her feel like she was exactly what everyone else had always said she was—an imaginary friend.

To make matters worse, I was in the middle of the road in front of my house, yelling after someone that no one else could see. And then, if you could imagine putting the cherry on top, I looked up and saw that my mom had been watching the whole thing from the kitchen window.

Shit, again.

It was the only word that could come out of my mouth at that point, so I just braved it and walked inside.

"Hi, honey. How was school?" Mom asked. I was sort of shocked by her greeting. Maybe she hadn't seen that whole thing play out. Maybe she only caught the very end and thought I was yelling to one of my friends from the neighborhood.

Probably not.

Then it came.

"That really looked like something a sane person would do," Mom said to me. Her words dripping with sarcasm.

"Not now, Mom," I said with an attitude.

Nope, she saw it all.

I walked to my room and "quietly" slammed the door. I did that when I was mad. That way, Mom had no idea I was making the motion of slamming it, but I got to feel like I was releasing some of my frustration. It usually helped.

This is just great. Our league championship game is hours away, Essi is furious with me, and now I have to deal with my mom, too? Could this get any worse?

I was talking aloud when I realized I was talking to myself, and while someone on the outside would say that happened often, I was really doing it this time.

I was insane, or at the very least, headed in that direction.

Essi is actually driving me insane.

My mom knocked on the door but did not wait for my answer. She just came in. That was a common practice for her, and I hated it. I wasn't able to keep it in any longer.

"Mom, gosh! You can at least wait until I say come in or something. I can't stand it when you do that. What if I had been changing or something?"

Her reply was nothing shy of embarrassing. "Oh, honey. You forget that I looked at your naked body for at least the first decade of your life. Trust me, it's nothing I haven't seen!"

She grinned. She found great humor in telling me things like that.

I felt steam releasing from my ears, but my mom didn't care. She just came in, sat on the floor next to my bed, and got comfortable.

I could see the pity on her face. I knew she wanted to talk to me about *her* but didn't know what to say. I could tell this was like the start of a conversation that happened when you break up with a girl for the first time. That's what it felt like, only it was my best friend, and no one could see her. I did not want to talk to my mom about this. She would not understand, but I knew she would try anyway.

"Derek, honey? You wanna talk about it?"

"No!" I snapped.

"Derek, I know I have not always been the easiest to talk to about Essi, but I want you to know that you can talk to me about anything. I mean that."

"Thanks, Mom, but no, I don't want to talk about it. I have to get ready."

She used the bed to help herself up and said, "Just because I can't see her doesn't mean I don't know what she's thinking. I know women, so if you decide you want a little insight into our minds, I will be in the other room."

She kissed me on the forehead and walked out.

That was the last thing I wanted to be worried about before the championship game, but my life was a complicated one, even at 14.

I put my headphones on and started to put my stuff together before my friend Tommy and his dad arrived at my house to give me a ride. I had a few minutes left, so I started to write Essi a note in case she came by while I was gone.

Essi,

Please don't be mad at me. I didn't mean it to come out the way it sounded. You know I know you are real. You are the realest thing in my life. I just wish other people could see you the way I can. I know that's not an excuse, but sometimes it's hard for me, and it will be even harder when you are gone. No one will ever be able to replace what you are to me, so if you are worried that I will love them more than you, it's not possible. Please come to my game tonight. It won't mean nearly as much if we win if you're not there.

I'm sorry.

<3 D

I read the letter to make sure it sounded right, and I was suddenly experiencing a heart-wrenching feeling I had never felt. Abruptly, I was sick to my stomach. I felt like vomiting, and my heart was beating so fast that it felt like it would jump out of my chest. I put my hand over my heart, wondering if I was having a heart attack.

But I realized it wasn't a physical heart attack but an attack of the heart, nonetheless. In an instant, I knew I was feeling something only people who had felt this could understand. It couldn't be explained in words, and I didn't know why I had just figured it out, but I had. Re-reading the letter had altered something. Seeing it on paper somehow made something click.

I was head over heels in love with Essi.

This complicates things.

On the way to my game, my mind did nothing but occupy itself with thoughts of Essi. That was normal, though. I thought about Essi all of the time, but this time bore no resemblance to my thoughts of her before. This time, my fondness was of a more mature manner. Suddenly, she had such an amazing smell that I couldn't breathe in deep enough to try and recall. Suddenly her skin was not pale anymore but milky white, and all I wanted to do was graze it with the tips of my fingers. Suddenly, her hair was as soft as silk, and all those times she asked if she could teach me how to braid her hair made me wish I had never declined her offer. I could actually feel my fingers running through it. I wanted to grab it, pull it even. Suddenly she had boobs.

Holy shit, she has magnificent boobs!

How had I not noticed them before? They were perfect, 100% proportioned to her tiny frame, just enough there, and now all I wanted was to know what they looked like uncovered, with the air touching them. Better yet, with me touching them. I started to yearn for her in a way I never thought.

I knew this was a normal thing to go through for a kid my age, but I thought I was supposed to be fantasizing about supermodels or pin-up girls, not Essi. This felt weird. And somehow, I was shocked that I hadn't come to this conclusion before. She was perfect in every way. It was like she was *too good to be true.*

I have loved her for 11 years.

In seconds, I went from being on Cloud Nine to Earth. I had profoundly screwed this one up, but my attention was needed elsewhere. We were playing in the state championship, and I needed to focus on that.

Tommy tapped me in the back seat and asked if I was okay. He said I looked flustered.

You have no idea.

From the time we arrived at the gym and all throughout warm-ups, it was all I could do to not search for Essi in the crowd.

I knew she was mad, but deep down I hoped I would see her sitting next to my mom in the front row. The seat stayed empty, and my mom was none the wiser.

Sports weren't really my mom's thing, but she yelled at the referees as if they had been. She made it a point to be at every game, which I was so grateful for. I think a part of us could feel my dad there, too. He would have never missed this game, and for her to be there was a badge of honor she wore proudly.

As the game started and progressively got more intense, I thought less about Essi and put all my energy into playing. Our team had been anticipating this game for weeks, and I was surprising myself with how well I was playing. At times throughout the game, our efforts seemed futile, but we battled back from a 13-point deficit in the fourth quarter to give ourselves a chance. Don't ask me how the ball ended up in my hands in those last few seconds, down two points, but there I was, the clock dwindling, and the crowd counting down.

"Three, two, one, shoot it!" I heard my coach scream.

I pulled up, and let it go. I watched in slow motion as it arched its way toward the hoop, bouncing once off the rim, and dropping right through the center of the net at the buzzer.

Hitting that buzzer-beater to make us league champions was a rush I had never felt. I had never been the hero before, and I loved it. Only one person could have made that better.

I wondered if she had made her way to my house and if she'd read my letter. I wanted her to know how sorry I was, but then there was so much more to say.

Am I really going to tell her?

How?

As my teammates and I huddled around, cheering and dancing around our trophy, I looked up, and I saw her. For the very first time, I actually *saw* her, and my heart dropped.

This changes everything.

We made eye contact, and I could tell she was still so mad at me, and everything in me told me to run after her, but I was a stupid adolescent boy, so I didn't.

It was one of my many mistakes regarding her.

She was waiting for me in my room when I got home, letter in hand, and before I could get a word out, she hugged me. I could feel myself start to panic. We had hugged a thousand times before, but it was the first time I touched her after knowing what I knew. I managed to free myself quickly, and I don't think she noticed, but there was a tingling sensation in every extremity of my body. All I wanted to do was reach for her again.

I told her I needed to shower and change, and we could talk after, but she said she had to get home.

"I'm sorry, too, and I'm so proud of you. Congrats on your win."

She had nothing to be sorry about, but Essi was like that. She always took accountability when she didn't have to.

She left, and for the first time, I ached for her return.

I need a cold shower.

Chapter Four
(Derek)

The day came—the day we had been avoiding and dreading for so long. We knew it would come. We had known since the beginning, but when you have years and months left, it's easy to sweep a deadline like that under the rug... until it's not, and the proverbial rug is gone.

My first high school dance was the Sophomore Winter Formal, the day before I turned 16, and I was so nervous. I had asked Jaqueline Grant to be my date, but that was only because I couldn't just show up with my invisible one. At least having a visible date gave me the facade of being somewhat normal. Up until that point, when it came to girls, I had gained a reputation of uninterested.

However, it worked out perfectly because Jaqueline wanted to be at the dance with me about as much as I wanted to be there with her. In fact, she made that perfectly clear.

"Derek, the only reason I'm saying yes is to make Andrew jealous. Don't even think about trying anything. I'll just stop you in your perverted thoughts right there. The answer is no."

The thought actually made me laugh out loud, which was not amusing to Jaqueline. She was by far the most popular girl in our school, and although I had become somewhat popular myself, little did she know the only person I would ever try anything with would be Essi. I knew if there would ever be a time for that, it would be that night while I still had the chance. I played it out in my head for several months about how I would tell her, how I would somehow try to convey my feelings, and every time I tried, it was like my tongue stopped working, and I had no voice anymore. I would get these knots in my stomach that would make me want to throw up, the kind you get when you have to tell your parents you have done something wrong, and you know their reaction will be pure disappointment.

Seeing Essi every day and having those thoughts was absolute torture, but the thought of losing her before it was time was more torturous than anything I could fathom.

Since the day I figured out how I felt, I vowed to keep it to myself until I could be clear she felt the same way. I read the lines and in between them but could never differentiate if she loved me as a friend or more. So, I said nothing.

That day was different. It was my last chance, and even though I knew it could change nothing and everything, I had to do it because she was going to walk out of my life no matter what I said.

That was it. I would tell Essi I loved her, and I would kiss her for the first and last time before it was too late… if she'd let me.

My mom got home from picking up my tuxedo from the rental shop. She honked outside as she pulled up, and we went to pick up the corsage for Jaqueline. Florist Florian was the local florist everyone used, so it was like a mini-reunion in her shop as everyone else picked up their flowers, too. As a few of our friends gathered in the lobby, talking about their dresses, suits, and shoes, my mom was chatting with Florian. We had known her family for some time, so she and my mom talked while getting our order ready. She complained that a few people had canceled their orders last minute, but the flowers had already been prepared, so she was frustrated about seeing them go to waste. On a whim, I sort of yelled, "I'll take two!"

Both Florian and my mom looked at me sideways, and I'm certain my mother bought no part of my story as to why she needed to spend double the money, but I told her they were both for Jaqueline, that she had two choices for a dress so I needed to make sure I had the color that would match either one.

Impressive lie.

I really just wanted to make sure Essi had one as well.

I think my mom was just so excited I was finally going to a dance, so she went with it, despite her doubt.

Florian gave us the second one for free since it had already been paid for, and we left to go home.

Jaqueline got the free one.

When we got home, we were a tad later than I expected, so I had to hurry and get ready. I ran upstairs to get in the shower, and my mom called up to me and asked if I would wait in my room for a minute. I was rushing, so that was annoying, but I waited in my room, per her request.

She's definitely up to something.

She knocked, and like normal, without permission to come in, she opened the door. "Close your eyes," she said. I rolled them at first, and then I obliged. "I know you think you spent your money on renting the tuxedo, but I really wanted this to be a surprise, so the people at the shop just let you believe that. Keep your eyes closed," she instructed. "Here's your $150 back. Use it on something important."

She placed the money in my hand. All of a sudden, I could feel her close to my face. No doubt she was making sure I wasn't peeking. I chuckled.

"Mom, they're closed. I swear."

"Open," she said.

I opened my eyes and immediately felt tears running down my face. Mom was holding Dad's favorite suit that she had altered so that I could wear it to my first dance.

"The tux shop made sure we got all your measurements correct, so it should fit perfectly."

I just sat there, sobbing like a little kid, and when I mustered up enough energy, I got up and hugged her like I had never hugged her before. I think my emotions took her by surprise, but for a moment, she realized something more was going on. In any case, it moved her to tears too, and we just hugged.

Dad would have smiled at that.

My mom had no idea what that night was actually going to mean for me, but she had just fulfilled the only wish I had since my dad passed—that he would somehow show me that he was with me. I felt like only he could understand the magnitude of tonight. He was the only person who outwardly accepted Essi, and I know he would have been heartbroken with me that she was leaving.

That suit was the best gift my mother had ever given me, and even though she couldn't understand why, I would explain it to her one day.

I showered and went to my room. I just stared at the suit in admiration. If I looked half as good as Dad did in it, Essi wouldn't be able to resist me. The swag and confidence he had when he walked into a room wearing a suit were unmatched, so if I could have just a sliver of that, I was sure to be alright.

I started to get dressed, and with a rush of panic, I realized I could not remember where I had put Essi's gift. It was almost time to leave, and I wasn't going anywhere without that. Even though we said no gifts because Essi wasn't sure she could take it with her, I decided that on the off chance she could, I wanted her to have something from me to keep forever.

I would always be able to recall her face and smell... and her laugh. But once she left, she would have no memory of me at all. It made my stomach hurt to think about, but it was the rule. I didn't have much of an explanation behind the Parallel's rules, but I knew the gist of the main ones, not that Essi was really allowed to tell me those either.

I turned my room inside-out, but it was nowhere. I was at a loss.

What did you do with it, Derek?

I remembered clear as day putting the bag in my bedside table drawer, but it wasn't there.

Leaning in the doorframe, my mom stood, and knocked on the door. "Looking for something?"

She was holding the box in her hand.

Shit. Shit. Shit.

"I hadn't realized you thought so highly of Jaqueline, honey. This is a pretty special gift for someone you just started dating." The inquiry was almost accusatory, but that was a common undertone with my mom. She was doubtful at best, but I don't think she had grasped the true intention of the gift.

"We are not dating, Mom. It's just one dance, and it's not for Jaqueline."

The look of bewilderment on Mom's face was replaced with utter angst when she connected the dots. I could only imagine what she was thinking, but she said nothing and handed me the box.

"You look very handsome, sweetheart. Just like Daddy," she said. "Are you ready to go?"

Deflection was her specialty.

"Thanks, Mom," I replied without looking at her. "Yes, just give me a second. I'll meet you in the car."

I grabbed all of my stuff and headed out.

It was so embarrassing still having to be driven around and dropped off at places by my mom, but for a 15-year-old with an overprotective mother, there was not an abundance of options. Since Dad's accident, Mom didn't trust anyone else to drive me anywhere, so she always made herself available and had sort of become the town chauffeur among my friends and me.

The silence in the car was almost unbearable, and the elephant in the room was large and incredibly heavy. I knew Mom was itching to ask me about the gift, but she was afraid of the answer. I was certainly not going to offer information, so I just sat there and stared out the window. I drifted a bit, trying to picture what life would be like without Essi. It made my stomach drop into my feet.

Suddenly, I was jolted out of my daze when Mom broke the silence and blurted out, "Who's the necklace for, D?"

I sat there for a moment. I debated on whether to lie or just come out with it. I knew my answer didn't really matter because she knew the truth.

I just looked at her and took a deep breath.

Out with it.

As we were pulling up to Jaqueline's house, before I could get the words out, all she could say was, "Why now?"

I definitely didn't know how to answer that. This conversation was 12 or 13 years in the making, and my mother chose the one night when I had the littlest amount of time possible to ask.

"Seriously, Mom? I should be asking you the same question. This is a conversation for another day. Someday, I'll explain. I've gotta go. I love you."

I could tell she was emotional, but I couldn't decipher her emotions.

I got out of the car, but as I closed the door, Mom was already rolling down the window, calling out after me.

I turned around to brave the lash-out but was greeted with empathy.

"She's lucky you chose her, sweetheart," she said.

"No, Mom," I gently smiled, "I'm the lucky one."

Without another word, a very slight smile, and some sorrow in her eyes, she rolled up the window and drove away.

I closed my eyes and took a deep breath. I needed the tears that were welling in my eyes to be gone. I had to calm my nerves before the night started, but what I saw when I opened them did the absolute opposite. What I felt could only be described as a movie scene. Everything stood completely still. The colors around me faded to black and white, and the term "weak in the knees" was totally understandable now. All I could see was *her*. Essi was standing on the other side of the street with her hands nervously clasped together in front of her. She was wearing the most beautiful red dress I had ever seen, and her eyes were as blue as the sky. She stood out so magnificently that I was certain the rest of the world could finally see her, too.

I wondered what she was feeling. She seemed unsure of herself for the first time since I'd known her, and the vulnerability that I felt coming from her was both nerve-wracking and sexy as hell. My heart was racing, and all I could do was put up my hand to wave. I couldn't very well run to her and hug her while standing outside of my date's house. She knew that. In fact, she wasn't supposed to meet me until we got to the school a couple of blocks away, but I had never been happier that she didn't do what we agreed on. I hadn't seen her since yesterday.

She is a sight for sore eyes.

She touched the line of her dress and pointed to me, in reference to my suit, and with a small smirk and a thumbs up, she gave me her approval. No doubt, she knew what my mother had been up to. She mouthed "go," and gave a little wave. "I'll be here," she said.

I turned toward the house to meet Jaqueline.

"Oh, shit! I forgot," I said aloud as I whipped around and ran across the street. Essi had this what-the-hell-are-you-doing smirk on her face, but she didn't say anything. Out of the paper bag, I pulled out the corsage and gently placed it around her wrist. Coincidentally, it was a red rose to match her stunning red dress.

Touching her skin sent electric waves down my spine, but I took a deep breath and said, "There," and headed back to the house. With a profoundly childish grin on my face, I started the walk up Jaqueline's front stairway. Essi's effect on me was massive and overwhelming… and confusing.

I'm going to miss that.

My smile quickly wiped away when I saw Jaqueline standing in her doorway with her right hand on her hip. She was irritated, and I really didn't care. In fact, the only thing I could think of was that I had hoped she hadn't thought that smile was for her. Feeding her ego was not something I wanted. She had minions for that.

She looked pretty but didn't hold a candle to my real date. I was sure she would make her unlucky target jealous. The thought amused me.

"What were you doing down there? Nevermind, I don't want to know. You were probably practicing what to say to me to get me to agree to kiss you or something. Ugh."

"You caught me," I responded sarcastically.

I'm sure the interaction between Essi and me made me look absolutely insane, and yet somehow, Jaqueline skipped over that part and made it about herself. She was good at that.

She made sure I remembered the "rules" and said, "Well, I already told you, it's not gonna happen, so don't even think about it."

It was a staunch difference from the hundreds of rules I dealt with from Essi. But Jaqueline's rule was a rule I liked.

She thought much more highly of herself than I did, and truth be told, I wasn't sure why I chose her as the person to take. There were plenty of other nice girls to invite. Maybe it's because I knew it would mean nothing for the both of us, but she didn't know I thought that way, so it sort of backfired. It was a lose-lose for me anyway, so ultimately, I didn't care. There was one upside to taking Jaqueline, though. Her ex, Andrew, who she intended on making jealous, hadn't been the kindest to me up to that point, so the thought of pissing him off, even a little bit, held some power.

We went through the motions of giving the corsages, pinning the boutonnieres, and taking pictures, so they could be vainly posted all over social media almost immediately. I was tagged in ten photos before we got to the bottom of the stairs. Of course, I had been edited out of most of them, but the few I did make, I didn't look half bad.

Essi was waiting at the bottom of the stairs. She just winked at me, and we started walking.

Jaqueline lived just a block from the school where the dance was held, so instead of being dropped off by our parents, we walked. I offered to carry Jaqueline's shoes so that she could wear her dancing shoes, and with my other hand, I protectively held on to the box inside my pocket. With all these people around, I couldn't hold Essi's hand, despite the incredible desire to, so that was the next best thing. She never left my side, though, and that was enough for the both of us.

The dance itself was uneventful. I danced with Jaqueline to two slow songs, and she was whisked away by Andrew after he couldn't take it anymore. Her plan had worked. She was all smiles, and she mouthed "thank you" to me as he carried her away. Andrew didn't return the same sentiment.

If looks could kill...

Essi and I sat in a corner, sort of off-grid, quiet enough that we could hear each other but too loud for anyone to notice that I was talking to "myself." It looked like I was singing along to the music in the corner once my date had left me and all.

It was obvious neither one of us wanted to talk about what was going to happen. There was no brushing it under the rug or looking at a calendar and telling each other we still had time. There was no time anymore, and my heartache was intense. It made the air around us heavy and hard to breathe.

We sat there silent, in our own little world, for what felt like hours. I needed to find the words, but it was like they were playing hide and seek in my brain. I felt like she wanted me to say something, but I was so afraid our thoughts were going in different directions. My heart was about to be shattered into a million pieces no matter what, so I had nothing to lose.

It's now or never, Derek. Put up or shut up.

I grabbed Essi's hand, and I led her out of the cafeteria.

As we walked through the double doors, the song "One in a Million" by Aaliyah started to play and faded in the background. It was an almost perfect reflection of Essi and me, but "trillion" would have been more on point.

"Where are we going, Derek?"

"I need us to be away from everything. I have two hours left with you, and none of those people deserve any part of me while you're still here. I don't even know why I agreed to do this."

I was leading her to the gym where I knew no one else would be.

I was frantic and becoming more frantic by the minute.

As she followed behind me, she placed her other hand on my shoulder and said, "Derek, stop, it's okay."

I stopped in my tracks, turned around, and wrapped her in my arms. The sting in my nose was there, and my chest was so heavy. I could feel my shirt dampen where Essi's face was resting. She was crying, too.

In a faint whisper, I heard her say, "I would never leave you if it were my choice."

I knew that was true, but unfortunately, it made no difference.

I opened the door to the gym and escorted her inside. I knew no one would check in here until they locked up for the night, so we would be alone a little while longer.

The dance ended at 11, but we had until midnight. I told Mom that I was on the cleanup committee, so I needed an extra hour, and she didn't seem to question its validity. I needed the extra hour as if my life depended on it because, at the time, it really felt like it did.

The bleachers weren't out, but there was a small bench to the left of the entrance where we sat down. She started to talk about all of the funny things we had done growing up, and all of a sudden, we were lost in our memories with each other. We were reminded that we had grown up together, and the realization of that was pretty incredible. She asked me about what I thought my life would look like in ten years, and I wasn't sure, but I could tell she was yearning to be a part of it, so I tried.

"I think I'd like to help people, but I don't know how yet. I definitely want to be my own boss, so maybe a surgeon or something." We both laughed because I was so clumsy. There was no way I should be counted on for something so serious.

The laughter stopped, and silence took over again, followed by silent tears. I knew our time was dwindling, but I couldn't bring myself to look at my watch.

"How does this work?" I asked. "What happens now?"

"I don't know," she said. "I just know that I can't see you past midnight, and I know it won't be a good thing for me if we try and break that rule."

"So, are you gonna just disappear from right in front of my eyes or something?" I asked.

"No, D. You have to let me go."

Hearing her say that felt like someone was actually grabbing my heart inside my chest and squeezing as hard as they could.

How was I supposed to willingly let her go?

Letting go of my dad was the hardest thing I had ever endured, and this was about to tie it. Essi was the love of my life, and I had to let her go, never knowing where or why.

"I have something for you."

"Derek Ivey! We said no gifts! I don't know what I'm allowed to have. What if I have to leave it behind?" she yelled.

"This is worth the risk. I need you to have something from me. I need to know that it's possible, somehow, in whatever universe, that you'll know me, that I'm not the only one who has these memories. I know it's a stretch, but I had to try."

I pulled out the small white box and handed it to her. She looked up at me, and with her Essi smirk, shook her head from my defiance. She opened the box and immediately knew what it was and what it meant.

It was a necklace with a padlock charm I had handmade to fit the key my father had given me. On the padlock, I had a message inscribed:

You are my vision.

With you,

everything is possible.

Remember me. -D

She leaped into my arms and buried her face in my neck. I could feel her tears dampen my shirt again.

With one hand wrapped around her, I took my other hand and brushed her cheek to wipe her tears away. She looked up at me, and without a second thought, I leaned in and kissed her.

She's kissing me back! Holy shit.

She kissed me back, and I went numb. I felt like I was flying or falling, I couldn't tell which, and the entire world around us was blurry again. Time stood still for a few seconds, and if I could have stayed in that moment forever, I would have.

She pulled away just slightly and a bit out of breath. She kept her eyes closed and stayed with her forehead against mine.

"Why didn't you tell me?" she sighed with pain.

I don't know what to say.

"I didn't know if you'd feel the same way," I paused

"The thought of pushing you away somehow, before you had to leave, was worth my silence."

She kissed me again softly, and this time, she was the one doing the breath taking.

"I've been waiting for this for two years," she said.

Me too.

"And now I'll be searching for this for the rest of my life," I said. I closed my eyes, and the tears wouldn't stop. This time, she was brushing my cheek to wipe away the tears.

"It's time, Derek. I have to go."

She stood up, and I snatched her hand as if to beg her to stay, but I said nothing. I couldn't speak with my voice, only with my eyes, and she knew exactly what I was feeling.

She squatted and placed both hands on the outside of my knees. My eyes followed her.

"Thank you for a lifetime of friendship and love. You have given me purpose," she said.

I grabbed the box from her hand and pulled the necklace from its constraints. She swiveled around and sat on her knees. Clumsily, I fumbled to open the clasp.

We're running out of time.

With my hands shaking, I placed the necklace around her neck, and she turned back around. With her hand over the necklace, as if to protect it, she looked up at me and said, "I don't care what they say, Derek. I will keep this forever."

She kissed me on the cheek and walked away.

I was tongue tied.

Wait! No! That can't be it.

I didn't even say what I wanted to say.

I didn't say *it*.

Derek, you idiot, stand up and go after her!

I looked at my watch.

It's not midnight yet. I still have a little time.

"Essi!" I called out after her. She stopped at the gym door but didn't turn around. "Derek, please, I have to go. You have to let me go," she said with a sorrowful, shaky voice.

"No, I can't, not without telling you something first."

I turned her around, grabbed her hands with both of mine, and kissed her knuckles.

"Essi Michelle Jackson, I have loved you since I was three years old. You have shown me a true and genuine friendship, and you gave me the honor of falling in love for the first time with my best friend. I am head over heels in love with you, and that will never change. I don't know how or when, but I feel it in my gut that we will find each other again someday. Until that day, you will stay in my memories and be alive in my dreams. I love you, Essi."

She gave me the infamous Essi smirk and said, "I loved you first, Derek."

We kissed one last time, and without looking at me, she hugged me and whispered in my ear, "I will never forget you. Happy birthday."

My heart ached with grief for the first time since Dad died, and just like that, she was gone.

I put my head and back against the wall for support, and suddenly, my knees weren't strong enough to hold up my weight. They gave out from underneath me, and I slid to the floor. With my knees pulled close to my chest and my head in my arms, I began to sob. I couldn't stop. Sadness had taken over.

With a jolt, I was brought back to reality. I had been enveloped in someone's arms, but I didn't need to look up to know whose they were. I knew that hug from anywhere.

Mom.

"She's gone, isn't she, honey?" she asked with kindness and empathy.

Through my tears, I said, "Yeah, Mom, she is."

And right there, in the middle of the empty gym floor where I said goodbye to my everything, my mom held me as I sobbed.

My life will never be the same.

Chapter Five
(Essi)

I just sat there staring at my dress. The moment I put this on, the clock starts, and my time with Derek will run out. Although we both knew this day was coming, I don't think either of us realized it would come this fast. For months, years even, we have been able to reassure each other that we still had time, and tonight, as I accompany him to his first high school dance, the day before his 16th birthday, the only assurance we have is there is no time left at all.

Tomorrow, I will wake up with no memory of him, and although I know somewhere buried deep he will be there, the memories we have together will be gone, and anything associated with our linkship will be gone as well. I won't even know to look for them or try to recover what is lost. Of the thousands of rules we have, this was by far the cruelest. And although they were put in place to keep us and our links safe and our world hidden, it really seemed like the main rules were completely out of touch with our realities.

They shouldn't apply to us.

I know Derek and I were a rare case. A bond with a link doesn't normally get to the 16-year mark. In fact, we were told it had been at least a generation since links were kept until that age, but once they knew we were different, that we would make it all the way, there should have been an exception to the rule.

I often provoked a conversation about the rules to my parents, asking painfully obvious questions—a futile attempt to get them to give something away, anything, but they always knew what I was doing. This morning was a last-minute Hail Mary, which did not result in a catch.

Yes, I know about football.

"Why can't I tell him? What will happen if I do?" I challenged them, even though I always knew the answer. The looks on their faces showed annoyance, but their bodies showed empathy.

Maybe they think the rule is dumb, too?

Mom and Dad always did a great job of advocating for me and explaining the ways of life here. I'm sure my willful disregard for the rules did not make that easy for them, but they were always quick to remind me of the consequences.

Derek.

"Sweetie, you know what's at stake."

"How could I forget, Mom? 'If I break it, I lose Derek' has been shoved down my throat since I can remember. Aren't there any other consequences? On Earth, when they do something, they're not supposed to as a kid, they get grounded for a couple of weeks or have their stuff taken away. Here, it's people," I yelled. "How can the Originators threaten to take him away from me when they're the ones who linked us in the first place?"

The decibel of my voice surprised all of us, and I got up and stormed to my room.

It's not fair.

I could hear them whisper about who would come after me, and after something like that, I could usually hear my dad's heavy feet walk up to my door.

He knocked, which was only a more polite way of telling me he was coming in, regardless of what I said.

I hear that's a parent thing.

"Oh, please, come in," I said sarcastically.

I sat there and listened to all the ways my dad tried to make sense of the rules, but nothing could convince me this was the right way.

Of course, I would abide by the rules as I had been told because there was nothing worth risking Derek, but why didn't I have a say? Why couldn't I just tell him to look for me? Even though I had no idea where we would end up, what was the reason I couldn't tell him to never stop searching?

Protecting the children we linked with made sense, but we're not toddlers anymore. Who was I really protecting at this point? The rules forbade me from even telling him that we can transition earthside, and I think that one crushed me the most.

He'll never know I'm there. And I'll never know he existed.

My parents were very secretive about where we'd go, but the rule was very clear: [*Parents of the linked will choose a destination and may not choose a dwelling in the same city as their child's link, or they forfeit their right to transition to Earth. Parents of the linked must also keep their destination secret from their child. A break in this rule will also forfeit their transition to Earth.*]

"Dad, I know you and Mom are just trying to help, and I love you guys for that, but nothing you say will ever make this right. In a few days, I know I won't remember or care, but I only have one day left with someone who is not just my link but the love of my life, and no matter how hard you try to make it better now, my heart is still going to break in a thousand pieces tonight," I sobbed.

For the first time, he did not try to convince me to follow the rules. He hugged me. "I know, baby. I am so sorry," he said with tears in his eyes. "I asked you a couple of weeks ago, knowing what you know now, would you choose differently? Has your answer changed?"

That was the easiest question yet.

No.

"No, Daddy," I said with the utmost confidence. "All roads don't lead to Paris; they lead to Derek."

We both giggled at the irony of my joke, and my dad left.

It really was the easiest question. No matter how much my heart would hurt after tonight, I would have chosen him. In a thousand lifetimes and a thousand different universes, I would always choose him.

It's time.

Breathe, Essi.

Fuck. It's not working.

My chest is so heavy. No matter how deep a breath I try to take, they're just not deep enough. They're short and empty, and they only make my heart race more. But he does that to me anyway, so it's a lose-lose for me tonight.

I'm not allowed to tell Derek how I really feel.

Yes. Another stupid rule.

For two years, I have waited for him to say something, anything. I have felt like things were different between us for some time, but still, he has said nothing. Sometimes, I can't tell if the difference between us is that I realized how I felt, and since then, it has been hard for me to be around him, or if we feel the same thing.

It has been confusing, to say the least.

I remember coming to that realization like it was yesterday. Since I was about three, we have been inseparable. He has been my best friend since the day I can remember... until one day, he was more, but I couldn't understand it.

I was so mad at him that day. He had started to play basketball again after his dad died. That was the worst time in his life. Mine, too. But I had been encouraging him to try again because I knew it would be a way for him to feel close to his dad again. What I didn't expect is that it would put space between us. I didn't know it would give him friends, "real" friends, or so he called them.

What the hell is that supposed to mean? "Real?"

I certainly thought our friendship was real but it's hard to explain to other people when no one else can see you. I mean, I kind of got it, but still. Those boys didn't have a clue about me, and I was his best friend.

Me!

They had been taking up all of his time, and it was like I didn't exist anymore.

I had been warned about this, though. The 16-year mark was rarely met because as your link grew, their ability to manage both worlds became more difficult for them. Even though I knew nothing would truly break our link, feeling like I was invisible to the one person that mattered most was earth-shattering, or I guess I should say parallel-shattering. His mom was the only other person I wished really knew I was there. She already thought of me as imaginary, but it was dreadful how much more invisible his mom could make me feel. Even so, through the years, despite the rules against it, I secretly always tried to leave her clues to let her know I was really there, especially after the accident. Whether she ever noticed or would acknowledge the possibility is a different story.

Nonetheless, I didn't care if his friends believed I was there. He wouldn't even try to tell them about me.

I'm jealous—rage-filled, mind-blowingly jealous.

I just wanted him to want to be with me. I knew it wasn't a realistic expectation, and when I was gone, I wanted him to have friends, but I didn't want to feel gone yet. I was still there, but at that point, I was starting to feel exactly how I was to everyone else in his world—invisible.

There was only one person in Derek's life that acknowledged my existence, and it took his dad a long time to do that. He even addressed me personally once—well twice, but that's for another time.

It was one of the best days of my life.

And the key that Derek wore around his neck was a constant reminder that his dad had accepted me. But he was gone, and watching Derek drift away to new people was more than hurtful.

We got into an argument the day of his championship game. I wanted so much to be there for him, but I was hurt. He knew I hated *that* word. Saying the word "real," as if it somehow didn't apply to me, was like I was being stabbed, but coming from my best friend was like being stabbed over and over again. So, I left. I knew his "real" friends would be there for him, so why did he need me?

I know I was being childish, but I couldn't figure out why.

I remember that I went back to his house to catch him before he left for his game. It didn't happen often, but when we fought, I felt empty, so I wanted to apologize. He was already gone when I got there, but he left me a note, and when I read it, all of my emotions were somehow clear.

My heart had been stolen, and there was no recovering it. I loved him, and it was not a best friend love anymore, although, of course, that would always be there. This was a jittery-hand, hole-in-my-stomach, sweaty-palms-kind-of love.

Suddenly, my thoughts of Derek turned from adoration to lust.

In a matter of seconds, I had just turned into a teenager.

This changes everything.

I went straight to the gym, and although I never told him, I saw his game. I saw him hit the winning shot and be the hero, and I was so proud. I also felt extreme sadness that I couldn't take part in his celebration. I wanted to run to his side and tell him I was there, but I wanted him to have his moment, too, and the people surrounding him at that moment would be there after I left, so I pretended that I only showed up after his big shot.

The way he looked at me at that moment was as if he saw straight into my soul, and he somehow knew my revelations from reading his letter. I was humiliated because it truly seemed that the way I felt would never be reciprocated. When he saw me, it was as if he felt sorry for me, but that didn't affect how I felt.

Everything changed for me that day. Anytime he hugged me or held my hand, it sent electric shocks through my body and put my mind into an altered state. I was in a constant state of blush around him after that point, and even though he didn't seem to notice, I always felt like he backed off after that.

I accepted that he wouldn't feel the same way, and I vowed to try and act as normal as possible. After all, I couldn't tell him how I felt.

He had to be the one to initiate an act of love, and he hadn't yet, so I wasn't expecting him to do it today. A girl could dream, but regardless, I was going to lose my best friend tonight, and I was in no hurry to get the evening started.

Derek and I agreed to meet at 8:00 pm at the high school where the dance would be, but knowing we had so little time left, I wanted to surprise him and meet him at Jaqueline's house. I was waiting on the opposite side of the street in front of Jaqueline's house when I saw his mom's car pull up. He looked a bit distressed and didn't notice I was there. When he got out of the car and was going to walk up to Jaqueline's house, I was about to whistle to him, but I saw his mom roll down the passenger side window and call his name.

"She's lucky you chose her."

Huh? Who's "she?"

He responded, "No, Mom. I'm the lucky one."

My heart dropped.

Is she talking about me?

Is she finally acknowledging my existence?

Wait, is she talking about Jaqueline?

Ugh, that's horrifying.

I wouldn't dare ask. If she were not talking about me, I would feel my heart break twice tonight. So, I left it alone.

She drove away, and he stood there with his eyes closed. He made me stop dead in my tracks.

Wow. He is sexy.

His dad's suit looked as amazing on him as I had expected, and I was so glad his mom picked up on my clue to get it tailored for Derek.

I wish I could run to him, but I can't. I only had a few seconds before he saw me, so I took him all in and captured a screenshot in my mind, hoping this image would never leave my memory. I knew better, though. The thought was unbearable.

He took a huge breath and opened his eyes, ready to take on the long night ahead of us.

Suddenly, he froze. His face went white, and for a second, I thought his knees were going to give out.

I'm not entirely sure what that was about, but it made me feel unsure of myself. I felt like a lost puppy. Was he mad I showed up early? Happy to see me? I couldn't tell.

My hands were clasped together and dripping sweat.

What is going on with me?

Put on your game face, Essi.

Get it together.

He waved. I looked up behind him, and Jaqueline was in the door, watching him.

I did not like her, and I know he didn't either, but she thinks everyone does. I could tell she was confused by his behavior.

I pulled at the top of my dress and pointed to his suit, giving him a thumbs up. He most certainly had my approval. I think he understood.

I'm so glad I could keep the suit a surprise because I almost let it slip a hundred times over the last few weeks.

I told him, "Go. I'll be here," and waved him along. I could see Jaqueline was growing impatient. He gave me a small smile and turned toward the house.

I relaxed a little and went to sit on the bench, just a few feet away, when I heard him say, "Oh, shit! I forgot." He turned back toward me and started to cross the street.

Holy shit. What is he doing?

Jaqueline is sure to have questions for him now.

As he crossed the street, he reached inside his little paper bag and pulled out a small flower.

With my hand over my mouth and the slightest giggle, I looked around to be sure no one else could see this, but I could see Jaqueline's confusion pile.

He grabbed my hand to put the small red rose around my wrist, and I felt like he sent my body into shock, like I had been thrown into ice-cold water and couldn't breathe.

I just shook my head at him with a smirk as he turned around and walked toward the house.

The swag is unreal.

I felt a bit dazed, and I couldn't figure out what was happening. What was he thinking? Even if Jaqueline were the only one watching, that would stir up some bizarre thoughts and questions. I know what that looked like, even from my perspective, and it would have been pretty weird.

To be completely truthful, I didn't care. This is my last night with him, and if weird is what it has to look like for us to spend time together, so be it.

He was at her door, and I could see the reaction from Jaqueline. I'm not certain of what she said, but it was sure to be self-absorbed and self-serving if it was anything like her normal conversations.

I waited on the bench for what felt like an eternity. Of course, I had the ability to go into the house and see what was going on, but I didn't want to be a burden to Derek with all of those people around. Not that I thought he cared, but after tonight, those were the people that would take my place. That thought grabbed at my heart.

After tonight…

After tonight, there would be nothing. I felt like my life was ending, and in a way, it was.

Not only will I lose my best friend, but I will also lose him without getting to tell him how I feel. I know it's not up to me, but the saying "no regrets" isn't possible because not telling him he's my person would be the biggest regret I'll ever have.

On the upside, I will wake up tomorrow not knowing what I've missed, and even though that thought, right now, makes me feel broken inside, I imagine it will be somewhat comforting tomorrow.

It's both the hardest an easiest choice I've ever had to make. Do I stay in the Parallel with only his memory or join his world without the memory of him in the hopes of finding him again someday? I know any chance of seeing him again is worth it to me, so that has already been decided, but these stupid rules won't let me tell him I'll be here, somewhere, and I'll be "real."

As discouraging as that is, and as high as the chances are against us, I know I will never allow myself to lose him, not completely. He will be stowed away somewhere in my mind, and someday, I don't know when or where, he will come back. I will never stop looking for him until he does.

The couples started to trickle down the stairs, and a pang of jealousy ran throughout my body when I saw Jaqueline link arms with Derek. He looked straight at me, and I felt a bit more at ease. I know what she was doing with him. Derek had really come into his own this year. Surprisingly, he had become the popular kid at school. Of course, he never really noticed that, but

I did. And it pissed me off that it took all these people so long to see what I had seen for 13 years.

I joined him on his other side and aggressively wished I could take his hand, but I just nudged him to let him know I was there. He gave me a side glance and smiled.

How does the saying go, "A penny for your thoughts"?

I wanted so badly to know what he was thinking, but I couldn't ask him. Not now.

He was obviously nervous and kept fidgeting with something in his pocket. This is his first dance, but I can't imagine him feeling nervous about being around Jaqueline. If his feelings are anything like mine, the anticipation of the end of the night is getting to him.

I know it's getting to me.

The walk to the school was long and nerve-racking but spending time with him in any capacity was good enough, so I was trying to enjoy the time.

The night felt long and drawn out. I know I was counting down the seconds, but truth be told, I was sitting in the corner for most of the night, waiting for our time to be alone. We were sitting alone quite a bit, but to everyone else, Derek was sitting by himself, and people in his class kept coming up to him to make small talk. I'm sure they felt bad for him, but they would never know that him going to this dance was as much a cover for him as it was for Jaqueline. Her plan worked gloriously, though. Her boyfriend, Andrew, wore his jealousy right on his sleeve and whisked her away the moment we got to the dance. He made sure Derek saw his disapproval, but Derek didn't care. In fact, I think he almost enjoyed that part. Seeing her genuine smile as he carried her off was actually pretty cute, but I still didn't like her.

We sat at the table in the corner for what felt like hours, totally silent.

I wish I could just tell him.

I know full well what the consequences would be if I say something, but really, how would anyone know?

But they always know.

I can't take the chance of never finding him again.

I looked at my clock and realized time was not on our side. If I was going to tell him, it had to be soon.

As if he somehow read my mind, he abruptly stood up, grabbed my hand, and led me into the hallway.

Holding his hand made me feel the intensity I was certain he would never feel for me. But none of that mattered now. Wherever we were going, I wanted to spill my heart and have no regrets, but how could I not regret losing him?

"Where are we going, Derek?" I asked.

His response stung.

"I need us to be away from everything. I have two hours left with you, and none of those people deserve any part of me while you're still here. I don't even know why I agreed to do this."

Why did we do this?

Whose idea was it to be here with all these... strangers?

Oh, yeah, mine.

I thought I was doing him a favor by making him go to his first dance. Plus, truth be told, the thought of him experiencing his first dance after I was gone and not being able to steal that memory was not an option. Still, it seemed all sorts of stupid now.

As he led me out of there, I could see he was frantic. He was almost running. I slowed us down and placed my hand on his shoulder.

"Hey, stop. It's okay."

In a flash, he stopped and turned around to hug me. His arms were wrapped so tightly around me. For a moment, I forgot about everything. And then, without any provocation, I was quietly sobbing on his chest. If things work as they should, I won't remember how this felt. I flashed back to all the moments that led me to love him, and I couldn't keep it in any longer. He was crying too, although I'm sure it was for completely a different reason.

He's losing his best friend.

I'm losing the love of my life.

I would never leave him if it were my choice.

He opened the door to the gym, where he led me to a small bench. It was dark and quiet and pretty perfect for the moments coming.

I really hope we'll be alone in here.

We sat down, and as we stayed there in silence for a few moments, I thought about so many memories between Derek and me. I blurted out my favorite one, and from there, it was as if we were lost in our own secret story. We had known each other for so long, and even though I could always dream of our future together, I couldn't picture it anymore as time dwindled away. It was fading to black. I needed something to hold on to, to be a part of his future somehow, so I asked him what he thought his life looked like in ten years.

A life without us.

That stings.

He told me he wanted to help people, and I couldn't think of a better path for him to take. He is so kindhearted and so generous with his time and love. Giving back in some way would for sure be his calling.

He mentioned the possibility of being a surgeon, and we laughed so hard at that thought. Derek was one of the clumsiest people I had ever known. I really didn't see becoming a surgeon in his story, but I would have loved to be a fly on the wall for his first operation.

Our laughter softened, and we became silent again.

Silence turned into tears for me, and they slowly started to sneak down my face onto the floor.

It's now or never.

My mind searched for a way to start, and just as I opened my mouth to tell him how I feel, he asked me the one question I couldn't answer.

"What's next?"

You're asking the wrong person.

Truthfully, I really didn't know. Of course, what I knew I couldn't tell him anyway, but I couldn't fathom how tomorrow was going to be. And beyond that, there were many secrets about where we'd go, and my parents were unwilling to loosen their lips on our pending destination. It felt protective in a way, but I couldn't get them to open up about any of it. The cutoff was approaching fast and even though neither of us really understood it, breaking that midnight rule would be bad for everyone.

Even though all I want to do is break that rule.

"So, are you gonna to just disappear from right in front of my eyes or something?"

I'm not a magician.

He knew he had to let me go, but telling him that was so painful.

How can I ask him to do that when it's the opposite of what I want?

In fact, it's the absolute last thing in the world that I wanted, but if it gives me half of a chance to get back to him someday, I would pretty much do anything.

I know what I'm asking of him. I watched him lose his father.

For weeks, I watched his turmoil, day in and day out, and I can't imagine what this will do to him. Moreover, I can't imagine not being the person to console him. I couldn't help but hope that his mom had gotten my clue that I was leaving. Although when it came to me, that's all she ever wanted. I knew she'd show up for him if he needed her.

There were many times I watched his mom sit in Derek's room when he wasn't there, so I was hopeful this night would be no different. I made sure I placed his calendar wide open on his bed after they left. He had circled today's date in big red ink and wrote: "*She leaves.*" His mom was good at connecting dots, so I was optimistic that if she saw that she would know what to do.

I watched him for a few seconds and tried not to picture him being sad. He reached inside his pocket and pulled out a small box.

"I have something for you," he coyly said.

"Derek Ivey! We said no gifts!" I yelled at him.

He knew there was a chance I wouldn't be able to take anything with me, so we had agreed not to give each other anything. I knew I would love whatever was in that box, but if I had to leave it behind, I would be devastated.

I can't bear that thought.

"This is worth the risk. I need you to have something from me. I need to know that it's possible, somehow, in whatever universe you're in, that you'll know me, that I'm not the only one who has these memories. I know it's a stretch, but I had to try."

He handed me the box. I shook my head at him.

You are infuriating... and adorable.

I opened the box, and in an instant, I knew what it was. His father had given him a key before he was killed, and on that key, his father told him that he believed I was real. It was the only thing we ever had that made us feel less crazy.

He made a lock to fit his key and put it on a chain to be worn as a necklace, just like his. It read:

You are my only vision.
With you,
everything is possible.
Remember me. -D

The request was torturous and painful to read, but there was nothing I wanted more.

Without a thought, I leaped into his arms and hugged him. I started to cry again, only this time it wasn't silent. He just held me.

Time is running out.

It's now or never.

He grabbed my face and brushed away my tears with the gentlest touch.

That's different.

He guided my face until our eyes met.

His eyes looked different all of a sudden. He was looking at me in a clashing contrast from his normal stare.

What's happening?

My heart started to race, and my breath was short. If he had looked down, he would have seen my hands trembling, but his eyes never left mine.

Do it!

I was begging with my eyes.

Show me you love me, too.

Everything with me is possible, remember?

Do it!

And in a swift second, he was kissing me. I was paralyzed. All the air in the room and my body left, and it was as if gravity no longer existed. We're floating. I'm sure of it.

Fucking finally!

I kissed him back. Hard.

Time was at a standstill.

Let's just stay here.

All my fantasies over the last two years had finally come to fruition. Well, not all of them.

Idiot! Why didn't you say something?

I know my face said it for me, but I had to ask anyway.

"I didn't know if you'd feel the same way," he answered.

Of course, I did, dummy!

This whole time, we could have been doing God knows what.

Don't go there. That's dangerous, and there is not enough time.

Neither of us could bear the thought of losing the other, so a tortured misery of teenage emotions was the result. It was endearing and ever so maddening.

No! We missed so much.

But that didn't matter. All we have is now, and I'm not going to waste it on what might have been.

Kiss him!

I grabbed his face, trying to memorize it with my fingers, and I kissed him, again.

Jesus.

Everything in my body is on fire, and I unexpectedly became less cowardly.

I need him to know everything.

I had been waiting for this exact moment for two years, but despite wishing for time to stop, I had less than ten minutes to embrace a once-in-a-lifetime love.

I was wiping away his tears, taking all of him in, and then it hit me harder than ever.

11:53.

"It's time, Derek. I have to go."

I stood, and Derek snatched my hand abruptly. He looked up at me, and his eyes said everything I ever wanted him to say.

I squatted down, and with both hands, gently grasped his knees. His eyes followed me.

I love his eyes. I will miss them.

He had given me purpose and the most genuine of friendships, and I thanked him for that.

He grabbed the box from my hands and fumbled to get the necklace out.

He wants to put it on you, dummy. Get down!

I swiveled and kneeled.

He swept my hair to the side, and the touch to my neck made me shudder.

11:56.

Hurry!

His hands were shaking, but he placed the necklace around my neck and clasped it together.

With my hand over it, I turned to him and made a promise I had no intention of breaking.

"I will keep this forever."

Shit.

I kissed his cheek because I knew anything more would put us past midnight.

He was lifeless, and I knew I had to leave.

11:58.

"Essi, wait!" he pleaded.

No! There's no time. You have to let me go.

"No, I can't. Not without telling you something first."

He walked to face me, grabbed my hands with both of his, and kissed them.

My heart is breaking.

"Essi Michelle Jackson, I have loved you since I was three years old. You have shown me a true and genuine friendship, and you gave me the honor of falling in love for the first time with my best friend. I am hopelessly in love with you, and that will never change. I don't know how or when, but I feel it in my gut that we will find each other again someday. Until that day, you will stay in my memories and be alive in my dreams. I love you, Essi."

He loves me—the words I dreamed of hearing him say since reading his letter.

My world is rising and collapsing at the same moment, and it isn't fair.

11:59.

You better tell him back and fast!

"I loved you first, D."

We kissed one last time, and without looking at him, I hugged him and whispered, "I will never forget you."

How could I?

He will be impossible to forget, and for the first time, I know that's true. I will make it back to him.

With all the power left inside me, I mustered enough strength to push through the double doors.

I started to run.

Don't you dare look back.

The doors closed behind me as if to cut the link to our worlds forever.

And with the stroke of midnight, my heart shattered into a thousand pieces, taking my legs with it. The grass didn't do much to soften my fall. My body met the ground with force, but that wasn't the pain I felt. I just laid there and sobbed.

Out of nowhere, I was up in the air and cradled on a familiar chest.

Daddy.

The tears were heavier now, and I just let go. Through my sobs, I heard him say, "I know, baby. I'm sorry. It's unfair right now, but you'll understand someday."

No, I won't!

How can they do this?

I was too tired to say how I felt and too sad to do anything but cry, so I just let him carry me home.

My mom was there waiting, holding the door open.

I met her sorrow-filled eyes, and I knew she could feel my broken heart.

Moms always know.

Dad carried me up the stairs to my room. He gently set me down and said, "Mom put out something comfy for you. Get changed. I'll be back in a sec."

I stripped off the dress and put on the sweats and T-shirt my mom had set out for me. I grabbed the box of tissues, climbed into bed, and stared at my dress for the second time today.

When would be the next time I would go to a school dance? Or would I?

Would this dress bring back any memories?

I need to keep it. And the necklace. I'm keeping them both!

My dad knocked, peeking in the room to make sure it was safe to come in.

All I wanted was to see Derek, to make sure he was okay, but having my dad there took some of the stings away. I nodded for him to come into the room.

"I wish I could see him," I sobbed. "He's all alone, Daddy."

"His mom was there, honey."

Oh, thank God.

"Really?" I asked for reassurance.

My dad's nod gave me the only sense of relief I had all night.

"Surely, he has you to thank for that."

My blushing and sheepish face was the only verification Dad needed, but I didn't need to justify why. He knew.

My head hurts.

He sat on the bed next to me and started to rub my forehead the way he always had when something bothered me.

"Daddy, I need to keep the necklace," I pleaded as I showed him what Derek had given me. "And I want to keep the dress. Please. I need to keep them."

Dad sighed. "I'll find a way, baby. I promise."

I don't know if he was going to keep that promise but the confidence in his voice was enough for me to feel at ease about it.

With tears still streaming down my face, I started to doze.

I'm tired.

"Get some rest, sweetie. We have a long few days ahead of us."

And then my dad leaned over me to kiss my forehead and whispered, "Don't worry, kiddo. We'll help you find him."

Wait, what?

Open your eyes!

Did you hear what he said?

I tried to tell my mind to stay awake, but I couldn't. I was hijacked by exhaustion.

I sleepily uttered, "What are you talking about?"

But I couldn't wait for the answer. As my brain powered down, I heard him whisper nine words that changed everything. "How do you really think I met your mother?"

Holy shit.

Derek.

And that was it. I couldn't hang on anymore. Darkness came, and sleep took over.

Two days later...

I woke up to a rainy day and couldn't tell morning from evening.

What time is it?

Better yet, what day is it?

I felt like a had been hit by a truck. My head was pounding, my body ached, and when I stood, I almost fell right back on my bed. I was off-balance.

Why?

My parents must have been at the door waiting for any kind of noise because they both came right in and stood there staring at me, with weird smirks.

What's going on?

Why are they looking at me like that?

"What's wrong with you guys?" I asked.

"You hit your head on Friday, and you haven't been feeling well the last couple of days, so we wanted to come in and check on you," my mom said. "So, how are you feeling?

The last couple of days?

"What day is it?" I asked.

"It's Sunday, honey. You've been asleep since Friday."

Friday?

Something important was Friday.

No matter how hard I tried to remember what had happened on Friday, I couldn't.

Did I have a big test or something?

How have I been sleeping since Friday, and I don't remember?

Something incredibly weird is happening.

Amid the headache, my mind felt cluttered, but I couldn't organize my thoughts. It was like I was reaching inside my brain to grab at memories, and even though I felt them there, they were out of reach.

My parents were still in the room, both still staring at me as if they were searching for something. I could not tell if it was playful or serious, but something was up.

"Seriously, what's going on, guys?"

"Nothing, honey. We swear," Mom said. "We're just worried about you."

I looked at my dad, and he confirmed what she said.

"We just wanted to check on you and see how you're feeling. I'm sure the stress of the move didn't help, but hopefully, all that rest has done its job." Mom paused for a minute and then said, "By the way, your new principal called. They are very excited for you to start this week."

New school?!

Move?!

I knew it was something.

It was all coming back to me. We chose to leave the Parallel and transition to Earth, and I was super stressed about everything.

I was so nervous about starting at a new school.

Being the new kid in school is the absolute worst.

We had to come up with a story about where we came from, and the entire explanation was a bit numbing. At this age, when it is no longer possible for us to be in contact with a link, we get to make a choice—stay or come to Earth. I wanted to include Mom and Dad in the decision to come here, but no matter what they said, that would have been my choice.

I felt this unbelievably compelling urge to leave the Parallel. I don't know why, but it was like I was being pulled to Earth.

I had no recollection of my link, but that was how it was meant to be. I've never seen it get to the infamous 16-year mark, but I've heard whispers of it happening once or twice—nothing more than rumors, though, nothing to back them up, so I doubt they were real. That was the point, though. Remembering our links would just mess things up. It would interrupt the very essence of what they believe to be "imaginary friends."

I do wish I could remember something about mine, though. I imagine my link was a girl, and we were the best of friends. She probably forgot all about me, though. Most of them do. Links start to lose their "imagination" around six or seven, and that's probably when mine happened, too.

It's better this way, though. Feeling forgotten is probably pretty lonely. I would never really know whether I was forgotten, but now, per the rules, I was the forgetful one. I wonder at any point later in life if memories of my link would surface.

That's a good question to ask Mom and Dad.

I can't really say how I'd feel about that. Perhaps that would be too painful to stir up. Not all linkships end on a good note, but then again, what if I had one of those amazing ones?

My thoughts were wildly running in all directions, and with my new school starting Wednesday, it was probably better to go back to sleep. I didn't feel tired, but I needed my brain to shut off. Life as I knew it was about to begin and end in a way.

I'm the new kid.

Will I make friends?

Probably not.

Chapter Six
(Essi)

Six months later...

Life had slowed down quite a bit since moving. I could finally breathe a little. I felt like I could have chosen a better time of year to move schools, but I made a couple of fast friends, and once summer came, we were spending lots of time together.

I showed up at Beaverton High School just after Winter Formal. I had already learned the customs and cultures of Earth, so being out of the Parallel wasn't much different. It was like being here, only links didn't realize we existed right next to them. It wasn't so bad acclimating to life here and pretending to be one of them but getting people to like me was tougher than I thought.

We moved to Beaverton, Oregon, home of the biggest shoe and athletic company in the world. I love my sneakers, but I don't know why we moved here. My parents were very secretive about why they chose Beaverton. At 16, however, you don't get much say in adult matters. My dad just said it was work-related, so we moved. I have to say that Oregon grew on me by the day. It was a bit dreadful in the winter, as far as weather goes, but from what I heard, one must experience all the non-summer months in the Pacific Northwest to know just how dreadful. Summers, though, I could handle just fine. It was nothing but blue skies and perfect 80 to 85-degree temps every day.

It's funny, though. All I ever heard from people when we first moved here was how they wished it would stop raining, and they just wanted to see the sun again. Once the sun came, all I ever heard was how hot it was, and they wished it would rain again. And then, when it rains, no one uses umbrellas.

Oregonians are special.

Blake and Roxie were pretty special, too. On my third day of school, they came and sat on each side of me at the lunch table, introduced themselves, and started asking all sorts of questions. I was sure they were on some sort of dare, but it turned out, they just felt bad and thought it might give me a little relief from the anxiety of being the new kid. Eventually, they told me they had both been new kids as well, and even though Roxie was newer than Blake, they knew what that felt like and wanted to help. Plus, they told me they thought my name was really cool, and that alone piqued their interest.

The rest was history, really. After that, we were like the fearsome threesome. Although no one actually feared us, more so avoided us than anything, I appreciated feeling like I belonged in a group of friends. I don't remember ever having that.

We weren't overly unpopular, but we just kind of kept to ourselves, and that was okay with us. I couldn't quite understand why they weren't more popular, though. They were funny as hell, absolutely gorgeous, and total jocks. You could hear all the boys talking about them every time we walked by, but they didn't give any of them the time of day.

Blake was unique. She exuberated happiness, but I could tell she was holding on to sadness on the inside—probably why she didn't let many people in. It made me feel like I needed to protect her. She had this thick, wild, curly bleached-blonde hair that most people would kill for, but she hated it, so it always went in this crazy bun on the top of her head that she called a fun bun. I knew someday she'd be able to embrace it, but at the time, the fun-bun it was.

She loved golf, and she was really good at it. Her dad wished she would love it more, so I'm sure she was rebelling a little bit when she skipped practices for "cramps" or whatever excuse she could devise. She was expected to get an athletic scholarship to play golf somewhere, which was a pretty big deal, but the way things were going, I wasn't sure she'd still be playing by that time.

Roxie was confident, borderline cocky, but she pulled it off in a way that made you feel confident about yourself just by being around her. I noticed that about her right away. She had this air about her that gave the impression she wants people to stay away but makes it impossible for people to do that. She just kind of sucks you in. She's a total badass. She's a boxer and a softball player and has never been one to shy away from a little bit of bragging. Her dream was to move to Hollywood and be an actress, but I had never seen her do any acting, so I was pleasantly surprised when she auditioned for the lead in our school's rendition of *Grease*. She killed it!

In any case, I was very fond of them, and I knew they felt the same about me.

Blake, Roxie, and I were inseparable.

Each summer break, we rotated sleeping at each other's houses. I'm sure all of our parents were ready for school to start each year, but none of us were ever quite ready.

Being the new girl at 16 was tough, and I would never have survived without them. High school was so much easier with them by my side. Although we do not live near one another now, we make it a point to see each other as often as we can, and we have remained best friends since the day we met almost nine years ago.

One of my favorite memories with them was high school prom, and oddly enough, it was my first and only dance. I was voted Prom Princess, which I never thought would be possible, as I wasn't even sure anyone noticed me, but both Blake and Roxie were voted as well, and I was sure that I was voted in from pure pity.

We were each given a title. Mine was Princess of Intellect, Blake was Princess of Verbosity, and Roxie was Princess of Physique. Of all of us, Roxie's title made the most sense. I'm still trying to figure out why anyone thought of me as an intellectual. Pseudo intellectual, maybe.

I always knew what dress I would wear to prom if I were asked. Mom and Dad had kept this beautiful red evening gown when we moved, and without ever really sharing the story behind it, they always said it had a lot of significance. When I put it on, I shared the same sentiment. It felt important, but I could never give that feeling a reason.

I went to prom with James Dorsey. He was every girl's dream. He was so beautiful. He was tall, athletic, captain of the varsity basketball team, and super smart. What made him most beautiful was his kindness. He was so sweet.

When he asked me to be his prom date, he made this grand gesture in front of the whole school at our spirit week assembly, and although I was mortified, I most definitely did not say no.

I was a bit nervous about the prom, though, because I knew James liked me. My friends had been telling me for months, but all I ever got from him were hellos and side hugs in the hallways, so I never thought that meant anything. Then, the grand gesture of him asking me made a lightbulb go off.

Oh, he does like me.

Do I like him?

I couldn't tell if I liked him back. Blake told me, "You'll know," which was horrifying, but Roxie was the opposite.

"Just see how the night goes," Roxie said as we were talking on speaker while we got ready. "Maybe you guys will kiss, and you'll feel something, or maybe more!"

Whaaaaaat?

Kiss?

More than a kiss?

Oh, Jesus, help me.

"Plus, if you get crowned, you have to kiss your date anyway."

If she could have seen my face, she would have known I was looking at her sideways.

"What?" she questioned as I remained silent. "I don't make the rules."

I had never kissed anyone. I never really had the desire to kiss someone. My best friends were far more experienced, though. Some of their stories were even cringeworthy, maybe causing my reservation, but they assured me that being intimate with the right person was amazing.

We'll see about that.

Normally, we would've gotten ready together, but our dates weren't going in the same group, so I planned to meet them at the Trade Center, where the prom was held. As a part of the Prom Committee, Roxie had been setting up all day and didn't have a whole lot of time to get ready anyway.

I was so excited to see them in their dresses. Roxie chose a very deep V-neck gown with as little fabric on the back as it did in the front, no doubt to show off her amazing physique. I remember her saying, "We have to give the people what they want."

We laughed so loudly in the dressing room that the manager came and asked us to lower our voices. It sent us into a giggle fit, of course, which the manager didn't like… until he realized Roxie was buying the very expensive dress.

Blake chose an elegant one-shoulder teal dress. It had these amazing gemstones underneath the bodice that looked like it was made for a princess, so it was very fitting.

I took a deep breath and slipped on my dress, a ruby red, A-line mermaid gown that made me feel like a goddess. I looked in the mirror and felt an intense sense of déjà vu, but no matter how hard I tried to grasp what had already been, it was outside of my reach.

The doorbell rang.

Shit.

He's here.

I walked out of my room, and Mom and Dad were waiting, being as awkward as possible and camera-ready.

Good Lord.

"Stop!" I said as quietly as possible. "Oh, my God, you guys are so annoying."

"One picture, honey, please," Dad pleaded while showing me his new iPhone. Mom just stood there with her hands in front of her lips and tears in her eyes.

So dramatic.

"Ugh. Fine. One picture. James is waiting," I said as I smiled for the camera, then rushed to the front door where James was standing.

Woah.

He looked so hot. He had on a black tux with a red bow tie and cummerbund to match my dress and black kicks with a red bottom.

You would.

Oregonians were serious about their sneakers, especially in Beaverton. It was definitely a badge of honor around here that the world's biggest sporting company was from this very city.

I didn't get the memo to wear casual shoes, so my leopard-print stilettos had to do. It was better anyway, though. I was a whopping five feet two inches, and he was well over six feet tall, so I needed that extra height not to feel so tiny next to him.

It didn't work.

"Wow. You look stunning!" James said. "Princess Essi, I am honored to escort you to prom," he said as he held out his elbow for me to take.

"Thanks, James," I blushed. "You clean up well yourself," I returned with a smile and a red flushed face while accepting his gesture and looping arms.

He knew he had that effect on girls, but that hadn't happened to me yet, so I saw some satisfaction on his face when he finally had that effect on me, too.

And after an awkward silence with my parents creeping around the corner, I looked up at him and asked, "Time to go?"

"Absolutely!" James excitedly quipped.

"Wait! We need a picture!" Dad said.

I looked at them annoyingly.

"What? We need to have our daughter's first dance captured properly."

If this weren't my first and only dance, it'd be my only for sure, now.

We obliged and took the mandatory before-dance picture. It was probably better, though. By the time we took pictures at the dance, I had looked as if I hadn't done anything to get ready at all. My curls had fallen out, my makeup had faded from all of the sweating, and my feet were killing me, so my shoes became an in-hand accessory.

Dinner reservations went off without a hitch, and James was pleasantly surprised when I did not order the obligatory salad. Instead, I ordered the filet. My dad always said that a great woman orders the filet.

Or wait... that wasn't my dad.

Who said that?

Hmm...

We got to the Trade Center right on time, and waiting at the front to greet me with giggles and hugs were Blake and Roxie. We spent the first few minutes fawning over how each other looked in our dresses, and once we got a few quick selfies out of the way, we headed in with our dates, although at that point, it was as if our dates didn't exist.

Sorry?

As the dance got closer to the end, I felt more and more nervous. I had danced with James, but not slow danced, and then there was the impending crowning. What was I supposed to do if I won? Would I really have to kiss him? In front of all these people?

Don't be ridiculous, Essi. There is no way you will get voted queen over all the other girls on the court.

Truth be told, I had no interest in winning. There were people way more deserving than me. I was just happy to be there and experience it with my best friends.

The music stopped, and we heard a familiar voice over the speakers. "Princesses, it's time! Make your way up to the stage for the crowning!"

Everyone cheered, and all of the princesses gathered on the stage. We stood in a line, squeezing hands so tight, waiting for the announcement.

The Prince of Intellect, Kris Pearson, or Kris-P as I called him, had been crowned Mardi Gras Prince a few months before at a dance I had not attended, as it was custom for the girls to ask the guys to that dance. You couldn't have paid me to do that. Well, Beaverton High School tradition allowed the prince to walk behind the princesses and eventually crown the winner. As such, Kris-P walked behind all of us, toying with the crown over our heads as he strutted. He walked back and forth, four or five times, making us wait even longer. The rest of our classmates were still cheering and whistling as they enjoyed watching each princess squirm in anticipation.

This is way more nerve-wracking than I thought.

The crowd quieted, and I realized Kris-P had stopped right behind Roxie and me. He hovered the crown over her head, as I expected, and she looked at me with a beaming smile.

It makes sense. She is the perfect queen.

Wait, something's up.

Kris-P quickly switched, and to my insane surprise, excitedly placed the crown on top of my head.

Wait. What?

No fucking way!

And in an instant, Roxie, Blake, and the rest of the princesses were hugging me and congratulating me, and the rest of my peers were clapping with excitement. I could not believe I was voted queen. Moreover, I could not believe how good it felt to win. That was a first.

My excitement came to a screeching halt when James tapped me on the shoulder to give me a congratulatory hug, and the whole crowd switched their clapping to a "kiss" chant.

"Kiss! Kiss! Kiss! Kiss! Kiss! Kiss!"

Oh, God.

I looked at Roxie, and with the funniest grin, she shrugged her shoulders, put her hands up, and said, "I tried to warn you."

Roxie knew this whole time. .

She did try to warn me, I guess, or prepare me was a better way of putting it. I clearly had not picked up on the clues.

James looked at me and asked, "What say you, Queen Essi?"

He leaned over and whispered in my ear, "If you don't want to, it's cool."

I just looked at him.

Ugh, don't be such a square, Essi.

Just get it over with.

I could have done a lot worse for my first kiss, so I went for it.

I grabbed his cheeks, pulled him into my face, and placed a small, simple kiss on his lips. It was nice, not really what I expected.

Why was I so afraid?

It was not what the crowd wanted, and they were boisterous about their disappointment in such a PG-rated kiss.

"Disney movies have better kisses than that! Come on!" I heard someone yell.

And in an instant, James had the palm of his hand on the base of my neck and the other on the small of my back. I lost the sense of gravity as he dipped me down and kissed me, like the end of a movie kiss when the unsuspecting girl gets crowned queen at her prom and wins the heart of the most popular guy in school.

Jesus, I'm a movie plot.

It did not take more than two seconds before I was kissing him back. My hands had found the back of his neck and had started to rustle in his hair. I was a bit lost, and I was startled when I felt something slimy try to slip through my lips.

Woah, is that his tongue?

Keep your eyes closed.

Yep. That's. His. Tongue.

Déjà vu ... again.

It wasn't as gross as I had imagined. It was kind of sexy. I could hear the crowd cheer even louder, and then as quickly as he dipped me down, I was back on my feet.

I felt a little disoriented and woozy. Was that the feeling Roxie had been talking about, or was that because all of the blood had rushed to my head?

I looked at James, and he gave me the smallest smile. I smiled back and stuck my head in his shoulder and arm to hide my blushing face.

The crowd had dissipated, and the music had started again. Only this time, a slow song was playing. James led me to the middle of the dance floor, where we had our first true dance. The song playing was K-Ci & JoJo's "All My Life," which would become our song. An oldie, but goodie.

He leaned over and whispered, ever so slightly touching his mouth to my ear, sending some intense feelings into my stomach, "I've thought about how that would be for months."

I pulled away just slightly to look at him and naively said, "Really?"

He sort of laughed and said, "Essi, you are adorable. How did you not know?"

I just shrugged, and he followed it with, "I'd like to do it again if you're okay with it."

I was nervous, but I gave him a small nod as permission, and he kissed me again. We stood there kissing as if no one else was around. I could still hear the song playing, but the chatter of voices had died down. I couldn't tell if it was because they had all stopped talking and were staring at us again, or if the world faded around us as it does in a movie in the final kissing scene. In any case, I enjoyed it far more than I expected.

Yep, they're staring again.

We left the dance holding hands instead of locking arms, and from then on, the halls at school weren't filled with his simple hellos and side hugs but flirtatious banter and small kisses in between classes.

James was my first kiss and my first boyfriend.

My first everything, really.

But no, not that.

We never had sex. I wasn't the wait-until-you're-married type, but I was waiting for something. I really liked James, but I knew I was never in love with him. I was in love with the idea of being in love, and that was enough for a few years, but as distance kept us apart longer and longer because of college, we used it as our way to grow further apart.

Let's just say I always knew something was missing. Something in the back of my head told me he wasn't the one. I'd never been able to figure out what that something was, but it poked at me often.

After we graduated from high school, James received a full-ride scholarship to play basketball at UC Davis, and I stayed in Portland to pursue nursing. I was so excited to be accepted to one of the best nursing programs in the country. And the plus was I got to stay home. Oregon Health & Science University (OHSU) was tough to get into, but I was up for the challenge. It always felt like my calling was to help people, but I really had this pull to be a nurse and never understood why.

I don't remember portions of my childhood for obvious reasons, but I always got the feeling it came from somewhere from that time. Despite the many times I had insinuated that, my parents never blinked at telling me it was just something I always wanted.

Mmmm, you're lying.

I was so busy in my program, and James was so busy with all of his training and travel that we didn't have time for each other. With basketball, he never got time to come home for Thanksgiving and Christmas, so it just felt like there was never time to reconnect.

The last time I saw James, he traveled to Portland State University to play in a pre-season game against the Vikings during our junior year. He took me to lunch at my favorite hibachi restaurant, and we sat there for a few hours just talking. It was nice, but I could tell he was getting up the courage to say something heavy on his mind. I always felt like he was more invested in us than me.

It turns out I was right.

It wasn't on purpose, but as I said, I just knew something wasn't right, and eventually, he could sense that, too.

He paid for lunch, and as I was grabbing my purse to leave, he grabbed my hand and tugged me back into my seat. His hands were sweaty, and I could tell he was nervous.

Uh oh.

"Essi," James said, still holding my hand, "I love you."

"I love you too, James... what's up?"

"I know you do," he responded, "but you're not in love with me, are you?"

Well, that's not where I thought this was going.

Without letting me answer, he said, "It's okay. I have known it for some time, and even though I wish I could spell you into it, I don't want that for either of us. And not in a bad way, but we both deserve to be happy. I mean, not happy, because I am happy with y..."

I grabbed his hand, and he took a deep breath of relief and smiled.

I smiled back and said, "James, you don't have to explain anymore," and then tears started to swell in my eyes. "I do love... I *do* love you, but if I'm honest, I think you're right. I think we both deserve more." And then the tears started racing.

"Ess, don't cry. Why are you crying? I thought this is what you would want?" he asked. "If it's not, tell me you're in love with me, and I will be the happiest man in the world."

I couldn't tell him that, and he knew it, but it seemed like he was genuinely okay with it. Maybe we had both accepted this was coming for a while.

"I just don't want to lose you," I said. "You've been such a huge part of my life here, and the thought of us not being close is… is just hard to think about," I sighed.

By here, I meant on Earth, of course, but he didn't catch that. I truly was sad to lose him. He hadn't done anything wrong, and he always treated me like there wasn't another soul around. By most standards, it should have been my happily ever after, but I knew there was another soul for both of us, so it was the right choice.

We left the restaurant, promising to keep in touch and remain friends, but as the story goes, that didn't last very long.

He still asked me to come to his basketball game that night. Of course, I obliged. I had not seen him play in person since high school, and back then, we weren't dating yet. Turns out, that night, we weren't dating anymore either.

I showed up to the basketball game early, and he grabbed my hand and introduced me to all of his teammates as his friend.

Well, that feels different.

They seemed as thrown off by it as I was, but he was quick to answer their impending questions so nonchalantly, "Essi and I broke up earlier."

I just stood there and nodded with a still face. I didn't know what to say, and I could hear all of his friend's kind of mutter and gasp.

"Um, sorry, bro," some of them said. They didn't know what to say either.

"No, it's okay, guys. It was the right choice. It was time."

Once they knew he was really okay with it, it seemed less awkward. I could tell that those guys knew a lot more about me than I knew of them, just like my girlfriends. Although I knew Blake and Roxie would be happy not to watch us Facetime ten times a day, they would be sad for us, too. After all, we lived together, and James had become a part of our group. They were fond of James, but I think they always knew it wouldn't last forever, at least Blake knew.

The guys got called back to the locker room, and I decided to take a walk around campus before returning to the gym to take my seat. There was too much time until the game started, and I did not like to sit for that long.

The PSU campus was in the heart of downtown Portland in what is fondly referred to as The Park Blocks. It was a beautiful campus with trees everywhere, but being that it was December, all the leaves had fallen, and it was just rainy and dreary. Winter months in the Pacific Northwest made you appreciate the summer.

I made my way back to the gym just before tip-off, and Blake and Roxie were waiting in the seats next to mine. I had forgotten they were going to be there. They instantly knew something was off, and I was so glad to see them. I sat down and told them what had happened, and with little to say, they just hugged me, and I knew they were sorry.

The mood of the night changed fast when they started picking out my next suitor in the stands and the game.

Well, that was quick.

They went through the program and started naming off guys on both teams. UC Davis was obviously off limits, so they focused on the Vikings. Even though they knew it wasn't in the realm of my thoughts, they thought it was a fun game, nonetheless.

"Ooh, he's cute. Look at number 42, Seamus McDade. Six feet seven. Hometown: Minneapolis." Roxie stopped Blake from going any further. "Next! She is not moving to Minnesota. He's hot, but he's out!"

We all laughed, and they continued naming players from the program.

"Jason Gianonni."

"Brenton Bing."

"Jussi Jones."

"Austin Moore."

As they rattled off their heights and personal information, I got lost in a daze, and their voices faded. I was listening, but more so watching James play. He was good.

What would my life have been like if I had told him I was in love with him instead of letting him end things?

Safe.

Yuck.

I didn't want safe. I didn't only want the friendship-type of love. I wanted a love that consumed my every thought—a love that is so intense it's unrealistic, the one you watch in movies and yearn to feel when you go to sleep that night. The one that makes you think no one else in the world could possibly understand how you feel, or anyone who explains this feeling is surely ripping the thoughts straight from your brain or heart. I wanted that.

No, I need that.

I was thinking about all the things I wanted that James didn't give me, and I could still hear Blake and Roxie shelling out details about Portland State's men's basketball team.

"Fred Zeno."

"Derek Ivey."

Woah.

"Wait, say that name again?" I asked Roxie.

"Who? Derek Ivey? Do you know him?" Roxie asked with excitement. "Ooh, do you know him?" she repeated.

"I'm not sure. It just sounds familiar. Which one is he?"

"Umm, let's see," she read from the program. "Derek Ivey, six feet three inches from Portland, Oregon. It looks like he's number 33."

"That one there," Blake said, pointing at him.

I was instantly questioning my sanity as to how I had not noticed him before.

Holy shit.

He is fucking gorgeous.

She pointed at the most beautiful man I had ever seen. He was all the things.

I studied him, and I couldn't find anything that wasn't sexy.

The phrase "tall, dark, and handsome" had to have been coined from seeing this man.

Native American, Hispanic, or Middle Eastern, I wasn't sure, but I was sure I wanted to meet him. No, I was sure I *needed* to meet him and find out.

He had tattoos everywhere and wore a jersey that was entirely too big for him, which was adorable, yet somehow, I could tell he was in shape. All I could think of was how I wanted to see what the rest of him looked like under his uniform and trace my fingers over every single tattoo, learning the story behind each one.

Jesus, calm down Essi.

He seemed cool, way too cool for me, but I didn't care. I was drawn to him. Whatever it was about him, I could not peel my eyes away.

Who are you, Derek?

In a matter of minutes, I somehow envisioned an entire life with this person—what I would wear on our first date, how he would propose, and that I would make him wait anxiously for my very obvious answer. I thought about which venue we would use for our wedding, what his reaction would be as he first saw me from behind the ivory curtain, and how we would be as in love as ever even after three kids. I was completely lost in my thoughts of someone I had never met and a life I would likely never know. It was exhilarating, scary, and ridiculous.

What is wrong with you?

It was as if we had known each other our whole lives, yet he didn't know I existed.

"Earth to Essi!" Blake laughed.

I was abruptly brought out my vivid thoughts by her hand smacking my shoulder.

"Take a picture, why don't ya!" Roxie giggled, but her eyes stayed on mine. "Ess, do you know him or something? What is happening?" she asked inquisitively with a slight smile.

"I don't know," I stuttered. "I've never met him, but I want to. Don't you? Good Lord, look at him, he is fucking gorgeous."

We all laughed, and my jaw shut quickly as Blake yelled out, "Go, Derek!"

Oh, my God.

He looked up toward us, and I pulled my hat down and quickly hid my face out of embarrassment. With my face cloaked underneath my hands, I said, "Geez! I cannot believe you just did that, Blake."

"What? You said you want to know him. I'm gonna make that happen for you," she replied

"No, not like that, beotch!" I snapped.

"Hey, no better time than now," Blake said.

Blake was like that, though. If there was something she wanted, she went for it. She was not shy in that department, and it usually worked for her. I, on the other hand, was shy. I mean, it took me months to realize James was into me, but this was different. I instantly felt connected to this Derek guy, and I could not for the life of me explain why.

I have to know him.

We sat and watched the game, and it took all the power in me not to just stare at him. I knew I was there to support James, but I was drawn to Derek. It was the weirdest thing. On top of that, he was very good at basketball. It seemed to me he was the leader on the team, like the captain, maybe. He commanded everyone's attention and sure as hell had mine.

Who are you?

Although I knew James was doing everything in his power to impress me, Portland State ran away with the win, and Derek ran away with my attention.

Coincidently, James and Derek guarded each other almost the entire game, and in my head, it seemed like they were in a duel over my feelings, only neither of them knew it. James had a good game and ended with 15 points, five assists, and two steals, but it was nothing compared to Derek's 25 points and eight assists. Shooting was clearly one of his strong suits because he went seven for seven from the three.

We waited for a few minutes after the game to say goodbye to James. Secretly, I was hoping to run into Derek. Maybe I could shake his hand and there would be no spark at all, or maybe it would send shivers down my spine. Just saying his name inside my head made me feel out of sorts. I couldn't shake this feeling.

James came to give us hugs and thanked us for coming. I let him believe he was my only thought, and even though it was incredibly awkward, I made sure to give him my full attention. I would have been horrified if my only chance to meet Derek was in front of him, so I made it a point to be sure that didn't happen.

After we hugged and he left, I made my way to the bathroom to upgrade whatever reflection was staring back at me.

Hat on or off?

Um, definitely on.

Blake called me and told me that the PSU players were making their way out, and so I started walking to the lobby of the Stott Center, where family and friends were gathering to greet them.

I was nervous, so nervous, and there was no explanation for it.

How could someone I never met make me feel like this?

I made it to the lobby, and I met two extremely disappointed faces on Blake and Roxie.

Shit. What's wrong?

Blake gave me a look-over-there look with her eyes.

I followed her gaze to where I saw Derek and what I could only describe as Barbie standing in front of him.

Of course.

The woman he was immersed in a moment with looked exactly like a modern-day Barbie doll. She was stunning. She had platinum blonde hair to her butt and a body to die for. She also carried around a tennis bag.

Of course, she is.

I wasn't even mad. How could I be? They were a perfect match. He was a basketball star, she was obviously some sort of tennis star, and I was… me.

I watched them with envy, and in less than a few seconds, my hopes were as deflated as an old balloon.

The way he looked at her was... everything. He held her face and stared into her eyes before kissing her. I would have thought it was adorable if I wasn't so disappointed. I couldn't bring myself to look anymore, and we left.

I acted as if I was fine, but I wasn't. In one day, I had lost a best friend, because you know how the lets-be-friends thing goes, and what felt like a love-at-first-sight moment.

I know it was very melodramatic of me. How can you lose a love-at-first-sight moment when the other person had no sight of you? But I couldn't explain it. We were connected somehow, and ironically, I thought that perhaps in a parallel universe that he would have seen me, too.

Sigh.

As the night crept away, so did my thoughts of Derek. Seven shots of tequila will do that to you.

Wait, was that tequila?

Blake and Roxie were determined to boost my mood, but they were trying to get me over my breakup. Little did they know that the reason I was so sad had nothing to do with James and everything to do with this Derek guy. My thoughts of him were heavy, but as we drank the night away, they felt lighter. Eventually watching the food I ate go into the porcelain bowl washed away my thoughts completely, or so I thought. I woke up in a cold sweat and my head was pounding from the alcohol, but I was more overwhelmed with a lingering dream.

That wasn't real, was it?

I was at a high school dance, I think. It still felt fuzzy. I was in my red prom dress that I wore with James, but this time I was in an empty gymnasium that I didn't recognize, and James was nowhere to be found. As I sat in the empty gym on the only bench situated by the door, I could feel I was in an important moment. My heart was racing, and my hands were wet, but I couldn't figure out why. I was heavy in my seat, and I couldn't move—the way dreams do that. But I heard footsteps approaching the double doors. I looked up and a person was standing in the doorway. The doors started to stretch far away from me, and I couldn't make out his face. I knew it wasn't James, but I did not recognize the silhouette. This person knew me; he reached for me, and as I instinctively tried to reach back out to him, the doors stretched further and further away, and as he faded into the distance, I heard him say, "Ess, remember me."

Remember you? Who are you?

He called me "Ess."

I wanted to lay back down to fall back into the dream, but as my body came back to reality, so did my spinning headache and the feeling that anything left in my stomach was about to come up again. So, I ran for the bathroom.

Shit.

I am never drinking again.

The sleep that followed was a result of finding the coldest spot on the concrete floor to lay my head, but my dream didn't continue. Instead, I dreamt about the basketball game from last night, and it was clear that Derek was heavy on my brain.

I watched him play in awe, and as the game winded down and he hit the winning shot, he pointed directly at me in the stands. I looked around and realized I was completely alone, but he was still pointing at me. As the buzzer sounded, Derek ran through the chairs and up the bleachers to me. He looked at me the way he looked at her. He was holding my chin the same way he did with Barbie. My dream before wouldn't let me stand, but this dream wouldn't let me speak. I was pleading with my eyes for him to kiss me. I wanted to know what his lips would feel like on mine, and just as he was about to kiss me, I was rustled out of my dream and awoke to a cold washcloth on my head with Blake staring at me.

"Jesus, Blake, what are you doing?" I asked with one eye open and a beating drum inside my brain.

"Well, you looked miserable, so I thought I should make you feel better. Only when I sat next to you, you started breathing all hard, and I thought maybe she's not as miserable as I thought."

My face turned red, and Blake's laugh turned from fun to inquisition.

"What were you dreaming about, you little hussy?" she playfully asked.

"Nothing," I responded. "Geez, my head is pounding. Would you just put the washcloth back on?"

She returned the cold rag to my forehead and sat with me. I could tell she didn't feel great either, but I was the one on the bathroom floor.

Roxie burst through the door and said, "What a pathetic threesome we are. Get up, both of you, we're going out."

And as quickly as she came in, she left.

"What?" I asked for clarification.

"Where are we going?" Blake and I called after her at the same time.

"Not telling. It's a surprise," she yelled. "We need to leave in one hour, so start getting ready."

I looked at my watch and shocked myself with the time.

5:30 pm?

I slept the whole day?

I jumped in the shower to try and shed some of my hangover, but the heat made my nausea worse, and I immediately had to turn the water cold.

Fu-u-dge. This is freezing.

That helped a little and gave me just enough energy to make myself presentable for a public outing.

As uninterested as I was in whatever we were doing, Blake and Roxie always made me feel better, so I obliged and allowed Roxie to continue with her charades. I figured we were going to grab drinks at the new lounge she had been talking about, but what I didn't know was there was a public event there for the PSU athletic program. "Meet the Viks" was a PR event where they would bring athletes from each of the PSU athletic teams to interact with the public and help bring more attention to the sports teams within the university. As we walked up, and I saw the sign for the event, I was completely mortified.

"We are not going in there," I quipped.

"Like hell we aren't," Roxie snapped back. "I heard you all night talking about Derek over the toilet bowl, and I figured we may as well just get this over with."

"Rox, he's got a girlfriend. You both saw the way he looked at her. There is no 'this' to get over with. Can we please find a different place to go?" I pleaded and looked at Blake to give me some backup.

She was absolutely no help.

She used the nickname they gave me in high school to ease the betrayal. Blake loved nicknames, so even though they liked my real name, they used my initials E.M.J. to come up with something just for them to call me. I liked it, but not then.

"Sorry, EmJ! I'm with Roxie on this one. What if he's the one who gets away? The way you looked at him last night made me want to go home and watch *The Notebook*," she laughed. "Being a part of this love story would be far too exciting to walk away from before you guys even meet."

"I hate you guys," I whimpered and bent my head back. They were not going to budge on this.

I looked at the stars for a few seconds, took a deep breath, and said, "Fine. With any luck, he won't even be here, and we can leave."

As we started to walk up to the line to get in, Roxie excitedly said, "Well, it's your 'unlucky' night, my friend."

I followed her gaze to the stunning man in the window of the lounge as I stopped dead in my tracks at the sight of Derek.

I let out a sigh and a moan at the same time. Suddenly, I felt nauseated again. The pit in my stomach made me feel like I had just been punched in the gut, and my chest started to become heavy.

Get a grip, Essi. You don't even know him.

I was melting and sinking at the same time. I wanted to retreat to the cold bathroom floor and spend my night over the toilet again.

Anything would be better than this torture.

I knew there was no way they would let me do that, so I put on a brave face, and we made our way through the line. As we got to the front, we could see people being turned away. In succession, we were met with an apologetic event planner, explaining they were at capacity and no one else could go into the restaurant. The smile on my face returned, but the girls looked at me with utter disappointment.

Bullet dodged.

"So, there's nothing we can do except wait and hope other people leave?" Blake asked.

"Yeah, unfortunately. I am so sorry. We did not expect such a big turnout, which is a good thing, I guess," she replied with a sheepish smile.

"Time to find somewhere else to go," I gloated. "I'm hungry anyway. Let's get some food."

Blake and Roxie both obliged and as we were starting the walk back to our car, I turned to the window where Derek was and was startled by an intense stare from him. He was looking directly at me, squinting and leaning forward as if to get a better look. I couldn't move from the spot I was standing. His gaze was stone cold and felt as if he was looking directly into my soul. I was completely frozen.

He bolted from my sight in the window and startled me out of my spell. I took my queue to catch up with girls as swiftly as possible. As we got in the car and pulled away from our premium Saturday night parking spot, I had this eerie feeling that I should turn around, but I couldn't bring myself to do it. I closed my eyes and clenched my purse, holding my breath for what felt like ten minutes. With the acceleration of the gas, it felt like Roxie could feel my haste, and as we took the freeway entrance, I finally let out my breath in relief.

"It's been a night, guys. Can we just go home?" I asked.

Roxie looked at me in the rearview mirror. We made brief eye contact, and it felt like she quickly understood I needed her accord.

"Yeah, I'm pretty tired too, now that I think about it," she lied. "We'll just head back to the condo. We can grab some food on the way."

I sat back, leaned my head against the cool window, and closed my eyes. It wasn't a far drive home, but my brain shut off fast and went into dream mode with the should-haves. And it couldn't have been more than one minute into my rest before Derek made his appearance.

Hello. You are going to be a problem for me.

Chapter Seven
(Derek)

Last night was one of the stranger nights I've ever had playing basketball, and I have played a lot. Noelle was pissed at me for something I couldn't control. Of course, I apologized anyway.

How could I help it if a bunch of girls we didn't know were calling my name in the stands?

I was pulled to look in their direction on more than one occasion but could never really get a good look at any of them, especially the one wearing the hat. She was familiar and mysterious, and I wanted to get a better look, but if I wanted to keep the limbs on my body, I knew I couldn't stare for too long. Noelle would have none of that. She was protective that way, and while sometimes it came across as jealous or overbearing, it was also one of the things I loved about her. I knew she loved me and would fight for me.

Like literally fight for me.

She waited after the game to make sure I knew she was annoyed. She masqueraded her ploy as congratulatory, but she didn't really care about anything other than letting everyone else know I was hers.

The team had already been giving me shit, asking about my mystery cheering section, and I walked out of the locker room to hear it from Noelle, too.

I grabbed her face, looked her in the eyes, and told her a gentle lie. "Elle, you know you're the only woman for me," and then I kissed her softly.

Saying that out loud sort of made me cringe on the inside, but I learned throughout the years since Essi left that telling your current girlfriend that your soulmate was your childhood imaginary friend, and they'd never compare, would never go over too well. The gentle lie was the better choice.

Obviously, there was only one woman for me, but no need in being unkind to Noelle. I did love her, and she really was wonderful, but the truth is she would never compare to the love of my life. No one ever would. And that wasn't her fault. I had accepted long ago that I would live my life with a relationship bar set so high it would be impossible to reach because of her.

Other than my parents, only one other person in my life knew the real story about Essi, and amazingly enough, he never made me feel weird about it. Joshua was one of the neighborhood kids who encouraged me to play basketball after my dad passed, and he quickly became my closest friend after Essi left. He knew something was off with me after my birthday that year, but I couldn't bring myself to open up about it. He tried to get me to talk, but I used my dad's death as my reason on several occasions.

It wasn't a lie because that would always bring immense sadness, but when she left, it changed me again, and he could tell. A year after her exit, on my 17th birthday, we went to a party with a bunch of friends, where I smoked weed for the first time. I don't know exactly how much it was, but I know with certainty it was entirely too much, and I ended up telling him everything. It was as if someone turned on a water faucet from my brain and memories of her just poured out of me. At first, I think he probably thought I was having a bad high or something, but he just let me roll with the stories. I am fairly certain I even cried when explaining how much I missed her, and he never said a word. As quiet as he was, I thought he had fallen asleep mid-story, but all the confirmation questions came the next day when he asked more about her.

Hmm. He was listening.

It is very possible, to this day, that he thinks I'm crazy, but if he does, he never told me. I'm sure he and my mom have talked about it in private and maybe had a few laughs over it, but in our many years of friendship, he never made me feel unheard when I spoke of her.

Josh has always been a great friend to me. Josh was funny, kind, and loyal. He had a wild personality, but only to those in his circle, which shocked people as they became friends with him. He was a great soccer player and quite the looker—your textbook definition of jock. He was never without his phone and always had multiple conversations with girls at the same time. I would just shake my head every time I heard it ding from an incoming message, and he would always look at me with the biggest grin and say the same thing, but a new name: "What? It's Sarah. She's just a friend."

You sure have a lot of friends.

Despite his inability to be monogamous, he was a great person and a better friend, and I always felt so much comfort knowing I could be myself with him. Essi was such a huge part of my life and having someone I didn't have to hide that from meant I could be my authentic self. He had a way of getting me to do things that pulled me outside of my comfort zone. I didn't always like that but appreciated it if that makes sense?

During our senior year in high school, he convinced me to go to prom, which I was totally against for obvious reasons. The last place I saw Essi was at a high school dance, and my heart had not mended, nor would it ever. Still, he somehow convinced me it would help with the healing process. He was careful not to use phrases like "forget about her," or "get over her," because it was clear that would never happen. However, he did bring up the point that I could insert new memories next to a high school dance, perhaps finding a positive way to look at prom instead of using it like a trip to drive down melancholy lane.

He was right.

I asked our friend Ashley because I knew she would not take it the wrong way. We lived in the same neighborhood nearly our entire lives, but neither of us ever paid much attention to each other growing up—not in an unkind way, I just never had time, I guess. When Essi was around, I didn't have much time for anyone but Essi. But once Essi was gone, acquaintances slowly became friends, and she was one of the few I had. I knew if I asked Ashley, it wouldn't mean anything other than going as friends, and for obvious reasons, Jaqueline would never be an option again.

I figured it would be the last time I would ask someone to a dance, so I did it big. I went for the full-fledged embarrassing "promposal" and asked her over morning announcements at school. "Ashley Monroe, will you do me the honor of escorting me to prom?" I paused and asked, "Please?" It was not a two-way speaker, so I had to wait until I got to our first-period class to get an answer.

She had written "YES" on a big sign and was holding it up when I blasted through the door. With a big fist pump and the obligatory acceptance hug, I had a date to prom, a pretty awesome one, I might add.

She was lots of fun to be around and knew how to be the life of the party, which was entirely the opposite of me. She was not overly popular, which I loved, but could be friends with anyone. She was a killer athlete and super smart, and I was fond of our friendship, so I was glad I went, even more glad that if it couldn't be with Essi, it was with her.

The dance itself was uneventful, which was a good thing, nothing at all like my last dance—also a good thing. When I think of high school dances, I can see clear as day the last time I saw Essi, but I can also smile at my memory of prom. Although it's a juxtaposition of emotions, it's better than just having the one from before. Both Josh and Ashley helped me with that, and I was grateful for their companionship that night.

I don't remember who Josh's date was because whatever love affair he was having at that time was fleeting, but I do have a great picture of the three of us from the dance that I keep framed on my fireplace. It goes wherever I go, serving as a good reminder that no matter how bad things feel, life always evolves, and I will always be okay. I never thought I would recover when Essi left me, but having those two were literal lifesavers for me.

The summer after graduation was wild. Amid all the craziness, Ashley and I may have attempted exploring if what we had was strictly friendship.

It was.

And turns out, Ashley and Josh realized after just one year apart that was the only time they ever needed to be away from each other. Who knew Josh could be tamed, and crazier that Ashley would be the one to do it? Now having experienced them as a couple for a few years, it's quite unbelievable we all didn't realize it sooner. They made so much sense—not in the "love at first sight" kind of way, but the "find your best friend and then marry her" type of way. There was so much balance between the two of them. I never really saw a lot of passion, at least not that they shared with the rest of us, but what I did see was genuine respect and love, and I envied that.

I probably envied it more because I had that once, but what I had was accompanied by incredible lust and passion. I realize now as I'm getting older that some of what I felt was being a hormonal teenager, but not the real parts. The 13 years of absolute inseparability were not because of puberty. Those were unconditional love. And as much as I envied what Josh and Ashley had found or grown, I knew I had found 100x more than that. I know most people have never experienced what Essi and I had, so I am beyond grateful to have had the chance of sharing that with her. We were just unlucky in our circumstances, I guess you could say, and not getting to experience it forever.

Forever is such a relative term. With the right person, forever can feel like it won't be enough time, but without them, it can feel like time stands still in the most unbearable way.

Without Essi, my forever is the unbearable kind.

Chapter Eight
(Derek)

Josh, Ashley, and I all chose colleges in Oregon which I loved because that meant we would keep in touch regardless of space and time.

Well, them especially.

My schedule was a little tougher once we graduated from high school because from the moment I committed to play basketball at PSU, it was all about training and preparing for my freshman year.

My dad would have absolutely lost his mind at the mere thought of me playing a sport in college, let alone D1 and earning a full-ride scholarship on top of it all. Of course, Portland State was no Pac12 or mid-major school, but going from never being interested in any sport at the age of 13 to taking official visits at not one or two but three D1 schools was more than an accomplishment to me. I knew I owed it all to my dad. Well, maybe not all of it, but he deserves a lot of the credit. The autonomy he and Mom gave me to find my own thing and excel at it was such a blessing. Many of my teammates over the last six or seven years were much better than me when I started playing, but I watched as a lot of them burn themselves out for one reason or another. I could even attribute some of my basketball success to Essi. I doubt I would have immersed myself so drastically into basketball had she not left, and I was definitely not losing interest because of a love life, which I watched unfold for a lot of kids my age, too.

Hormones are a bitch.

Regardless of how I got here, I knew I had a lot to be proud of, and being so close to home so Mom could watch and support me made it even better. Much like my dad wouldn't have missed a game, Mom never missed a game, including last night's. Ashley and Josh were there too, but they left before I could say hello. It was no secret they had intense feelings for Noelle, but not in a positive way. From the moment I brought her "home," so to speak, it was like the movie "Clash of the Titans"—too many large personalities, and Noelle never backed down from a challenge for my affection. Annoyingly enough, neither did Josh. He rarely shied away from an opportunity to tell Noelle a story from before her time—a dumb but very effective way for him to let her know he knew me better than she ever would.

My mom absolutely hated it, so she avoided those interactions as often as she could, and she was gone before I could say hi to her as well.

Noelle's ability to drive people away was unmatched, not always an attractive quality, but she got what she wanted, and in this case, isolating me was her intention.

She couldn't join me at tonight's event, and she was pissed about it. She and the tennis team were traveling for an indoor tennis tournament, and they left this morning. There was a little relief in being able to go by myself.

I loved her, but she was a lot. It's probably unfair of me to even date anybody, knowing no one will ever measure up, but I have also accepted that is my cross to bear, and I cannot forego potential happiness knowing the one person who gave me that will never be here. I have to try and find a different definition of happiness. Otherwise, what's the point?

I can't say that Noelle isn't that, but I can't say she is.

Me and my teammates met at the Stott Center to coordinate with the rest of the athletes for our big fundraiser, "Meet the Viks." We were bussed to this new bougie lounge in downtown Portland to rub elbows with the public and a bunch of rich boosters in hopes that they would give us more money than they already do. PSU is not like a lot of other D1 programs. We do a lot of our fundraising and never get as much respect as many of our Oregon counterparts. Despite being in the heart of the great city of Portland, PSU is considered a commuter school, so the athletic department fan base is usually limited to alum and family members of the athletes, but I love being a Viking. They are one of the few D1 programs that gave me a chance, so I am Viking for life.

I dreaded these types of events, but I put on a big smile, and I know how to work a crowd.

"Veronica and Darrel, I would love for you to meet the captain of our men's basketball team," Teri said. "This is Derek Ivey."

Teri Mariani was a lifelong Viking, having been a three-sport athlete and then the women's head softball coach for 30 years. Even after retirement, she helped at our athletic events, so she was more than happy to show two of these boosters my way.

I shook the hands of potential boosters and started in on my work.

Smile and charm, check. Here we go.

"It's a pleasure to meet the both of you. How can I help convince you that this is the school you want to donate your hard-earned money to?" I chuckled, and they followed.

"I don't think you need to convince us of anything. We have been fans of the program for years. In fact, you already get some of our money. We are just trying to figure out how much more of it we'll give.

Teri gave me an easy one.

"Perhaps I can introduce you to a few other of our amazing athletes to help add more zeros?" I chuckled again.

"Lead the way," Darrell said with a smile as he gestured with his hand.

I stopped mid-speech and stared out the window.

What in the actual fuck?

"Derek, are you okay? You look like you saw a ghost," Veronica inquired.

I think I did.

"Excuse me for just a second, please," I politely said.

Her gaze followed mine to the window, but without hesitation, she said, "Oh, sure, honey, take your time."

I walked closer to the window and tried to peer through. There was a heavy mirrored reflection so I couldn't be sure of what I was seeing, but the closer I got, the harder it was to believe that this was just a mind fuck.

Over the years, my mind has played tricks on me and showed me Essi's face, but this was different. She was looking at me through the window as if she knew me. She was beautiful and mysterious, and with the glare, it was so hard to tell, but I swear it looked like her.

Essi?

My mind was racing, and I squinted to get a better look. I knew it was impossible, but I had to see her in person.

Shit. No! Why is she leaving?

You better fucking hurry up before she gets away!

I bolted.

I surprised everyone around me as I sprinted through the restaurant. I bobbed and weaved through the crowd of wealthy donors, and amid the look of concern on everyone's faces, my coach called after me to be sure I was okay, but I knew I had no time. I briskly said, "Sorry, Coach, it's an emergency. I will be right back!"

Where did all of these people come from? Of course, it had to be tonight that we actually had a turnout. I'd never get out in time.

Finally, I reached the front entrance and used the bars on the front door to swing myself in the direction of where she had been standing.

No, no, no, no, no! Where did she go?

Fuck!

"Fuck!" I yelled in the middle of the street.

I started to run in the direction that I could only guess she had gone, but she was nowhere to be found. As I turned the corner of 10th Street, I could see a car driving away in the distance. I wanted to sprint after it to look this girl in the eyes, but realistically, I also wanted not to get arrested and to keep my scholarship. So, choice B it was.

With my hands interlocked behind my head, I took a deep breath of the fresh Portland air and made my way back into the lounge. At least if I had seen her, and it wasn't Essi, I would've had something to show for my erratic behavior. Instead, I made up a ridiculous excuse that I was nauseous and needed fresh air.

Ugh. He's not buying it.

The rest of the night was an outright success. We gained 12 new boosters and upped our current booster donations by more than $10,000. I also took home one of the coveted raffle prizes after Mr. and Mrs. Murrel put a weekend at their seaside vacation home as a big-ticket item.

A $10 raffle ticket for a possible weekend at the Murrel's beach front mansion? Easy investment.

Janet Murrel and her husband Robbie were distinguished alumni and diehard PSU athletic department fans, and they rarely missed an opportunity to show their support.

Even with the fact that I won a weekend away, which was a cool enough prize to have all my teammates trying to buy it off me, I couldn't shake the girl in the window. Her face, even with the glare of the reflection, was haunting me, and there was no way her ghost would leave me anytime soon.

I know her.

Who in the fuck was that?

Chapter Nine
(Derek)

I woke up to Noelle smacking me across the chest.

"What the hell, Noelle? It's the middle of the night!" I winced, rubbing my chest from the sting of her palm.

"Who in the fuck is Essi?" she glared.

My heart stopped beating for a couple of seconds, and I felt like the wind had been knocked out of me.

Shit. What'd I say?

A flood of dream flashbacks rushed back, and if I was talking in my sleep about this one, I was in trouble.

As slyly as I could, I tried to put the attention back on her, as if she misunderstood and heard incorrectly.

'Cause that always works. Idiot.

"Who? Noelle, Jesus, what are you talking about?" I tried acting surprised.

"Your dream, Derek! You were calling out to someone named Essi, saying you loved her. Jesus! I leave for two fucking weekends, and you are already having dreams of someone else? Seriously. What the fuck, Derek?" she screamed. Her fury was swift and painful.

"Good Lord, Noelle, a dream? You're mad about a dream? Will you please let this go? It's nothing, I promise. I don't know an Essi."

Not anymore at least.

"I don't believe you! Your words were intense like you knew her, and it felt pretty fucking real to me," she hissed. I could hear the shake in her voice, which was quickly followed by tears.

Ohh, don't do that.

"You have been so off the last couple of weeks, and now I get why. It's because of this Essi person, isn't it? Just tell me there is someone else. Don't lie to me. Don't make me the fool."

There will always be someone else, Noelle, and it's not your fault.

"Elle, it was nothing," I promised.

As much as I wanted to yell out what I was thinking, I knew I couldn't. If I wanted this to go in my favor, I knew I had to lie through my teeth. I needed to shove my thoughts and feelings about Essi to the side. That dream still had me reeling, so that was a challenge. It truly felt like we were at the lounge together, like when I went outside, what happened was exactly the opposite of reality.

In my dream, it was her. I walked outside, and there she was, waiting. She stood there with her hands tucked under her clutch and her arms twisted in a V. She had a short black linen dress and black strappy leather pumps with a ruby red heel bottom, and she was more stunning than I remembered. She had her head down but her eyes up as if they were waiting for me, searching to meet mine, and when they finally did, fireworks went off in my chest and my groin. I wanted to sprint to her, but when I called out to her, she had a look of utter confusion.

"Essi? Is it really you?" I questioned.

She was taken aback at the sound of her name as if she had never heard it from my mouth before. As if I had not said it to her thousands of times in the 13 years we spent together.

Perplexed, she asked, "How do you know my name?"

I felt like I had been stabbed directly in my heart with that question. I was beside myself at the thought that she didn't know me.

Has she completely forgotten about me?
This can't be real.
It's not real, you idiot. It's a dream.

"Essi, it's me, Derek," I answered, hoping that by hearing my name she would recall "us," that it would somehow help her remember everything we shared.

She said, "Derek," as if she was practicing saying it. She paused, and with a slight tilt of her head, said it again. "Derek?" It seemed like she was trying to find the reason it felt familiar to say my name but couldn't figure out why.

I started to walk toward her, and her eyes followed me. She tracked me around the car, the way she used to, until I was standing in front of her.

She had been gone for over five years, and despite my brain knowing this was a dream, I was not going to let her leave it without kissing her lips and telling her I loved her.

I was much more brazen than normal. Even so, my boldness surprised me. "Essi, I'm going to kiss you now."

She was so tense, but she just looked at me and nodded her head in the most vulnerable way, and I had never thought she was sexier than at that moment. I gently grabbed the back of her neck, pulled her in, and kissed her.

I remember this.

Half a decade later, it's exactly how I imagined it would feel. Her tension immediately released, and instantly, she was kissing me back. I felt her hands finally release the grip from her purse, and one of them made its way to the small of my back, sending a shock to all nerve endings in my body.

Please don't wake up. Please! I need this.

Our lips separated, and before she could say anything, before I had to hear her tell me she still didn't know who I was, I told her I loved her. "I loved you when you left five years ago, and I have never stopped loving you, not any second of any day since then. I will love you forever, Essi, memory or not."

I closed my eyes and waited for the rejection to come. Instead, as Essi was about to respond, I felt the sting of reality and Noelle's hand across my chest.

No! Wait! No! What the fuck? Ugh!

Somehow, after that dream, I was supposed to reassure Noelle that Essi was merely a figment of my imagination, an idea that I tried desperately to negate for 13 years. It felt like I was smearing her memory, and that thought made me resent Noelle a bit. But I knew I had to let it go if I wanted to continue any kind of intimacy with Noelle. I had to put on my big boy pants for this one. It took me a couple of days to overcome her jealousy and skepticism of a "no one" in my dream, but eventually, I won her over, and she was quickly back to being jealous and controlling over other dumb stuff.

I told Josh all about the encounter at the lounge and my dream. "Dude, it felt so real. It felt like we were really there in my dream together," I explained, "like the universe was giving me a clue that she's here and close. I don't know. I know it sounds weird, but it was so real," I exclaimed.

Josh's face was all I needed to know what he was thinking. It wasn't a face of judgment, but the face of protection. Josh was that way—fiercely loyal and a protector to his people.

"Derek, my guy. Don't you think if Essi was here, like anywhere in this world, that she would have come to find you by now? Like, you speak about this love as if Whitney Houston herself were singing about it, and yet you think she would have just left you wondering like that for the last five or six years? Nah, man. I would love to believe your greatest love is out there somewhere, but then again, it would be pretty shitty if she were because that would mean she's been here all along and didn't come for you."

His words stung my heart, but he was right. There was no way she wouldn't have found me by now. I was hopeful and gutted all at once. I knew it was impossible, and yet somehow, I couldn't shake the "what if" voice in the back of my head.

Dad always said I could do the impossible.

My hand reached for the key I was wearing around my neck. As I twisted it in my fingers and took a deep breath, I read it again. I had the strangest feeling that my dad was right there, reminding me of exactly what he had inscribed on it.

For the first time I was sure.

She is here somewhere.

I know it.

Chapter Ten
(Derek)

One year later...

"Hi, sweetheart," Mom answered the phone.

"Hi, Mom. How are you? I have some pretty exciting news. Can I tell you over dinner?" I asked.

"Sure honey," she replied. "That actually sounds perfect. I was going to ask you to come for dinner anyway. I have some news I want to share with you, too."

I don't like her tone or how that sounds.

I could hear the shake in my mom's voice, and my heart did a downward spiral to the floor.

Well, this conversation turned quickly.

This was her "he loved you so much" voice, and I knew only bad news was to follow.

"What's wrong, Mom? Is everything okay?" I asked.

The song "Sound of Silence" started to creep into my head, and I swear I could hear her tears dropping to her feet.

"Mom, please just tell me what's going on?" I begged.

"Derek, I—I need to see you, okay? So, I'll just see you for dinner. Tomorrow?"

It was a quiet demand.

"No! Mom, you can't do that! You have to tell me. Whatever it is, I can handle it," I pleaded, but I knew she wasn't going to budge.

"Everything is okay. I love you, and I will see you tomorrow."

And that was the end of that.

I couldn't even get out an "I love you, too" before she hung up. I just sat on the floor and played every horrible scenario in my head. I was a catastrophist at heart, so only the worst things I could think of were coming to the surface of my brain. It had only been me and Mom since Dad passed. What on Earth would I do without her?

Stop thinking like that! Jesus!

That night and the next day were absolute torture. I had knots in my stomach all day, and now, my exciting news seemed so far off and nowhere near as important.

I had decided to give basketball a chance after college. It was never really in my thoughts since I figured I would get my master's and begin my residency as a child psychologist. But basketball was presented as an option, and once it became one, it was hard to think about not trying. I knew if I didn't give this a chance now, I never would. I had the opportunity to go to the top professional league in Iceland, and it was a start to what could be a great career abroad. The money was shit, but I knew I would have to climb the proverbial ladder, no matter where I went, and with nothing to lose, I wanted to go for it. Plus, getting to see Iceland? Yes, please! I knew my mom would be ecstatic for me, but whatever impending news she was going to give me had replaced my excitement with angst..

I got to her house around 6:00 pm, and she was waiting by the door. Dad had always taught me that no matter where you were going to bring a gift, so as a small token from Dad and me, I brought my mom her favorite flower, a single bird of paradise with a small batch of baby's breath.

As I handed them to her, I said, "From me and Dad."

She cupped her fist to her chest and smiled. As she leaned over to hug me, she said, "Thank you, baby. It's beautiful. Your dad would be proud of the man you have become."

I could see her face was puffy, so I assumed she had been crying, but she wouldn't show it. My mom did not like for people to see her cry, so she was holding it together the best she could.

As she led me into the kitchen, to my surprise, Aunt Sandy was sitting at the table. She was always my favorite aunt, but we rarely got to see her because she lived in England and had been there most of my life. Aunt Sandy was the reliable one. If you needed something, anything, she was there to help in any way possible. I knew her being there was not a good sign, so I gave her a big hug, sat down, and braced myself for what was coming.

"Lay it on me, Mom. What's going on?"

My mom sat there for a moment, took a deep breath to speak, but cried instead. She looked at me as if to tell me with her eyes, and in an instant, I knew.

She's dying.

No. Please, God, no.

"Mommy?" My voice was breaking, and I looked between her and my aunt until someone spoke.

Aunt Sandy's head was down, but she grabbed my mom's hand and asked her if she wanted her to tell me. Mom nodded, and Aunt Sandy took a deep breath, looked up, and met my eyes with the sorrow that was filling hers.

"Derek, your mom has cancer."

The dreaded C-word.

"She is in stage four, and it is terminal."

No! This is not happening.

"Mommy?" I pleaded again.

Aunt Sandy waited about ten seconds and asked, "Do you understand what we are telling you, honey?"

No, Aunt Sandy. I'm a fucking idiot, and I don't understand my only parent left is dying.

Ugh, don't kill the messenger, Derek.

My head was spinning, and I wanted to crawl into a dark cave. I had so many questions but could only muster up one through my tears.

"You're gonna fight. You're gonna fight it, right?" I asked out of desperation. "You can't leave me, Mom. Please, I'm not ready."

She answered swiftly as she leaned over the table and grabbed my hand, "It doesn't look like there is much we can do, but I am willing to try anything. I promise, D, I will try whatever."

At least that thought was somewhat comforting. My mom was nothing short of amazing, and if anyone in the world could beat cancer, it would be my mom.

Four weeks before our dinner date, Mom had been diagnosed with ovarian cancer, and she was waiting for blood work and a biopsy to confirm its stage. She had already started treatment without telling me, and surgery was scheduled for the end of the month. Obviously, it was bad, but somehow, I felt like my mom would be around longer than she was anticipating.

What do I do now?

On cue, my mom was inquiring about my news, and it felt so much less exciting or important to share.

"Now that we have that out of the way, what was it you wanted to tell me? You sounded very excited, and I can't wait to hear. Give me something else to think about, my darling."

"Um, no. Not now," I said swiftly.

"Like hell you won't tell me!" she snapped back.

Yikes.

I looked at my aunt wide-eyed and surprised in hopes of some support, and all she could say was, "Well, I'd tell her if I were you."

Shit.

"Well, what I was going to tell you was that I got a chance to play basketball in Iceland. But it doesn't matter now. I'm not leaving, so there's that. Good talk."

My mom sat there for a moment in silence.

Fuck. She is actually thinking about it.

"If you think for one moment that I am going to let you stop living your life because my very full life might be close to its end, then you have another thing coming. I will outlive everyone if that's the case. You're going."

Even though I'd seen my exact hope in others crushed in tragedy, I was somehow blindly hopeful that my mom would be okay yet there wasn't anything she could say to get me to leave at this point. I wasn't going to tell her that. Mom loved to be right, so I let her think she had convinced me to go.

I tried to pretend I was hungry enough to eat, so I wasn't rude to Aunt Sandy about her cooking, but I just wanted to be in my mom's company. After a few hours, I could tell Mom was tired and ready to be alone, so I kissed her goodnight, hugged my aunt, and made my exit.

Mom never missed a time to wave to me in the window, so as much as I wanted to sit in my car and let it all out, I gave her the chance to wave me goodbye, like she loved to do. I made sure I was out of her sight before pulling over at the end of her street. The rain pouring outside matched the tears streaming down my face. The truth was, once my dad had passed, it never crossed my mind that my mom would, too. Of course, I was not stupid. I knew deep down she would die someday, but my brain had almost shut off the ability to think of losing her as well.

How can I live without them both? Without all three of them? Her too? No.

I was a cliché, sitting in the car, yelling, hitting the steering wheel, and crying so hard that I could no longer sniff in the snot coming from my nose.

Good reminder to grab tissues tomorrow.

I closed my eyes, and the overwhelming thought that came to me allowed me to take my first deep breath of the day. Somehow, no matter what was happening for me, if I thought of Essi, my body would feel calm, and all my anxiety would subside. Even after all that time, her effect on me was surreal.

I drove home in a fog, forgetting once I was home how I got there. I opened the door to a very empty place—cold and lonely, much like that cave I was looking for when my aunt dropped the news. Being home was not much different than that.

It was still weird walking in and not seeing any of Noelle's things, but it had been time for a while. It had only been a few months since Noelle and I had broken up, but my relationship with Noelle had ended long before it was officially over. The longer I pretended that Essi wasn't real, the worse it became to convince myself she was really gone. I could not shake the feeling that she was here somewhere, and yet, there had not been another dream about her since that night. I was foolish to keep chasing the thought, and eventually, Noelle felt foolish for sticking around. So, she ended things. She was not kind about it, nor did I expect her to be, but there was a bit of nostalgia watching her pack up her stuff and move out. I wasn't sure if it was because I was really going to miss her or that she represented the next best thing to happiness. Either way, the house felt lonelier without her, and not so oddly, more peaceful.

I graduated from Portland State with honors and a degree in child psychology. Pursuing that degree was fitting for what I had gone through as a kid. I wanted to make sure that no kid ever felt the way I did. I would teach and help kids embrace their links, or imaginary friends as we call them, never telling them they are not real. Because, truthfully, there is nothing worse for a child than not being believed. Of course, all my studies pointed me in the other direction, but I knew what I knew, and there was no way it wouldn't be a part of my eventual practice. However, the master's program and psychology side of me would have to wait.

After many discussions, borderline arguments, my mom finally convinced me to go after the opportunity in Iceland. She was in her fifth month of chemo and radiation by the time I left, and all signs were pointing in a surprisingly good direction. I made her promise if there were any changes that she would let me know immediately and she obliged. She really got me thinking about why I wouldn't go and what sort of things I would regret by not giving it a chance. Throwing my dad in the conversation and what he would think didn't help, but she was spot on. I could hear him say, "Will psychology always be there?" The most authentic answer I could come up with was yes.

But Mom might not be.

I knew there were few things my dad would have enjoyed more than watching me get a free education through sports, and watching me play professionally would have soared above that to the top of that list. He would have been in a state of shock.

Ultimately, doing something I knew my dad would be proud of and my mom's genuine permission were all the reasons I needed to say yes.

I was going to an old team in the top league of Iceland. There was very little information for me to go on, other than this basketball club had a lot of pride and history, and they believed the team they had built could help get them back to the top where they belonged. The city of Njardvik, Iceland, was just five minutes from the Keflavik airport, a drastic change from PDX.

When I landed, it was mid-September. It was drizzling, windier than anything I had ever experienced, and dark at 7:30 am. As the sun brushed the ground on its rise for the day, I could see the landscape of the country, and I quickly felt as if I had landed on the moon. There were no trees in sight, and the hills were trying to impersonate mountains. I had heard that Iceland was magnificent, but there had to be something here I wasn't seeing.

I was greeted by two friendly but unfamiliar faces—one was younger than me, but not by a lot, and the other could have been my dad. They held up my name on a white sign like I was a star in the movies, and I could feel an odd amount of ego oozing off me at that moment.

Stop it, Derek. No one cares.

I quickly centered myself and engaged with the two men who had picked me up—Agnar, or Aggi as he liked to be called, and Elli.

Elli was like a huge teddy bear and assured me if there was anything I needed at all, he was the man to talk to. He reminded me of the Godfather, the Icelandic Godfather. Aggi, however, seemed like he would be a really good friend to me. I immediately felt comfortable in his company, and it was a relief to have them both. The pang of homesickness and realization that I was thousands of miles away from my mom would have taken over without them there.

As we drove to my new apartment, and I soaked it all in, they gave me a very quick rundown of the town. In less than 30 seconds, we drove by all the important landmarks. The post office, police station, grocery store, pharmacy, and liquor store were all on the same street and closed on Sundays. Well, not the police station, although one could argue that as well.

I didn't like to go out much, but Aggi told me if there was ever a desire for that, I only had one option, and it was where everyone went on a Saturday night. Taxi was the name of the club.

"Unless there is a game, anyone our age will be there. Sometimes, Elli likes to show up too!" They both laughed.

"Yes, yes, it's true. I like to stay young and keep an eye on my guys, you know what I mean?"

Elli growled with laughter.

He had a very thick accent, but it was easy to understand his English.

Thankfully, I was not expected to learn Icelandic. I had no problem trying to learn the local language, but it was quite a relief to know that everyone I encountered spoke English.

As we got closer to my apartment, I was surprised to look out my window and see the ocean, which was less than 25 feet from me. I loved being from Portland because it was always so nice to have the mountains and the Pacific Ocean less than a two-hour drive in either direction, but this was the closest I had been to the Atlantic. I was even more surprised when we pulled up to my apartment and the ocean was still that close.

"Welcome home," Aggi said with a timid smile.

This is not what I had in mind when I wished I could someday have a house with an oceanfront view.

I let out a deep exhale, grabbed a suitcase from the open trunk, and Elli walked me up the stairs to the front door. Aggi followed behind with as much of my luggage as he could carry, and once everything was inside, they both gave me a grand tour of my new, two-bedroom, 800-square-feet apartment. It was fully stocked and ready for me, which was so nice considering the horror stories I had heard about overseas basketball. The apartment was newly remodeled, clean, and had nice new sheets on the king-size bed.

It was still the middle of the night in Portland, and I could feel exhaustion starting to take over once I saw the neatly made bed. I could tell Elli and Aggi had done this before, and they had quickly read my face and mind. They knew the only thing on my mind was sleep, and before I knew it, they were on their way out.

"Oh, and don't lock the door," Aggi said before he closed it behind him.

"Huh? Why?" I asked in confusion.

"Well, for one, there's no crime here," he shrugged, "but I will have to wake you up before practice, and since you don't have a phone yet, I don't have a way to get a hold of you if you don't wake up to an alarm."

"I would never oversleep for my first professional practice," I said with a bit of sarcasm.

Aggi laughed, and before he closed the door behind him, he said, "Trust me, every American says that on their first day."

Silence filled my new apartment, and homesickness was quickly making its way to the surface again, but I was too tired to acknowledge it. I changed my clothes and sat on the bed, and sleep took over quickly.

There she is.

Chapter Eleven
(Essi)

My first day was not what I expected. The expression "being thrown to the wolves" was an understatement; I was fresh meat. *If every 12-hour shift is like this, I don't know if I will survive.*

The first person to greet me was my new boss, Joelle, and although she was a bit curt and sometimes brutally sarcastic, I couldn't read her, yet I liked her. She was good at her job, intimidatingly good, but I knew I would learn a lot from her, so I tried my hardest to get in her good graces from the get-go. I can't say it worked, but I told myself over and over it wasn't me.

Nursing was an incredibly hard and fulfilling job, much like I've heard about parenthood. We are taught in nursing school to show emotion and be empathic, but there is a line. As much as I loved what I did, it took its toll. I was expecting to shadow people for at least a couple of weeks, but we were so overwhelmed and understaffed that I was immediately given rounds by myself.

If the dictionary used pictures as definitions, next to "fish out of water" would have been my photo. I can't imagine my patients didn't see that written all over my face, but they needed me more than my wish for treading water, so I went for it. Being in the oncology ward was not my first or second choice, but you go where the jobs are, and in the nursing industry, you don't look a gift horse in the mouth.

It was a great department, sad at times, as I knew most places could be, but it also had its overwhelming moments of pure joy. Watching my patients "ring the bell" was both thrilling and exhausting. Getting to experience a person re-see their future was nothing shy of amazing. It changed my perspective daily. Most importantly, I loved watching the ones who rang the bell and then left the hospital with the full intent to never take anything for granted.

Some of the best patients were the teenagers—the ones who've had a glimpse of the ugly side of cancer and still showed up every day with a mood that had nothing to do with their illness. The ones who had only just recently learned what love feels like and were trying to will their bodies into remission so that they could keep it or feel it again.

It was borderline devastating watching any of our patients walk back through our doors, but this was a sad reality, one that was quick to hit me in the face too many times in my first year.

Cancer was never talked about when I was growing up. It never made its way into conversations at home, and my parents might have sheltered me from anyone we knew experiencing it, but I was naive to its peril.

I hated what it did to people, but oddly, I also loved watching families, couples, friends, and their pets come together to support each other. I especially loved watching couples in their late stages of life, sitting at each other's side. I learned a lot about my patients in each 12-hour shift. And usually, by the time a person rang the bell, I could give a play-by-play of their lives and love stories.

It made me long for something similar.

Instead, I was a 24-year-old nurse, who was still a virgin, searching dating apps to find even the blindest of dates. James was the closest thing I had ever come to having sex, but I knew back then it just wasn't right. Thankfully, he was a gentleman about it. As crazy as it was for a girl my age in college to still be a virgin, it was even crazier for a guy, and James waited for me… although I heard he didn't wait long after we broke up.

I didn't care though.

I really wanted it to be special.

Deep down in my gut, I knew there was a connection out there so powerful that all the things before it would become obsolete. As much as I was tempted to mess with my cosmic plans, I didn't, and I was proud of that. I probably would have changed it all with that guy, Derek, from Portland State, but it seemed there were too many things in the way of what I deemed a connection. After we saw him at the restaurant, the girls pushed me hard about him for a while, and he heavily infiltrated my dreams for a good chunk of time.

I even dreamt that the night we saw him at the restaurant he eventually found me outside. He knew my name and details about me, which no one knew. In the dream, he acted as if we had known each other our entire lives, and just before I woke up, he kissed me like no one ever had. It was one of the most real dreams I can remember, but after that, I didn't dream of him again. Despite begging my brain to muster up new visions of him, to get lost in my reveries, they just weren't there, none that I remembered anyway.

I took it as a sign from the universe that he would never be more than a fantasy, and so a fantasy he has stayed.

Sigh.

Other than that, I was too focused on school and work to worry about a love life. My life was chaotic, and unfortunately, chaos and romance don't mix, despite the shit you see on television. My patients asked me daily why I wasn't dating, engaged, or married. Each time, I tried to come up with a clever answer.

"Why is it that no handsome man or gorgeous woman has caught your attention yet?" he flirted.

"Mr. Wiese, you know I'm waiting for you to leave the misses," I playfully responded.

Sadly, Mr. Wiese was a returning patient, but always entertaining, even when it was clear he didn't have much time left to entertain. He always got quite the kick out of our banter, but his wife, Claire, who was always sitting with him, would just shake her head and say, "You know all that does is give him an even bigger head, right?"

"You know I only have eyes for you, honey, so don't worry. EmJ isn't stealing me away that quickly," Mr. Wiese would say to make sure the attention turned quickly to his wife, which was something I admired. Despite it being clear that she did not need that kind of reassurance in the slightest, she was all too happy to accept it.

When I watched couples that had been together for decades, half-centuries even, it made me daydream and think about what that would feel like.

Does it get boring?

Is there lust after loving someone for that long?

Why don't you find lust for one month and stop worrying about lifetime shit?

Thoughts about finding love crossed my mind daily, and my friends were not helpful. Blake and Roxie only reprimanded me, telling me every time we spoke that I wasn't doing it right.

"Do you even try to meet people? I mean, for God's sake, there has to be some hot doctor or nurse there that wants to give you a good examination!"

They both laughed.

Am I blushing?

"Roxie, Jesus, not everyone can have the magic ability like you both do to entice every person they meet into giving them their number or IG page. It's actually unfair," I spouted back.

"Listen, beotch, it's easy to tell when someone wants to be left alone. You give off the vibe that you have either found your soulmate already or you never want one. Either way, you're covered in vinegar. No bees are going to approach you, okay? Be honey. See what happens."

They both knew how to "be honey." No matter where we were, they had people practically begging to buy them things and come home with them, and not always in that order. Blake even stopped giving her real name because they'd find her on IG so quickly it was almost shameful. I didn't know how to be any other way than me, but obviously, they were right, and my way wasn't working. I made a vow to try harder to give off the I-am-open vibe.

It was insane how fast it worked, which was just what I needed. In a matter of weeks, my newly unlocked persona helped me make two new friends, and they couldn't have come at a better time. I was lonely since the girls had moved, each having taken a new job in a different city. It just wasn't the same without them in Portland.

Of course, I always had my mom and dad, but they were regularly enjoying their hard-earned retirement, traveling as often as possible, and they were on the go when they were home, too.

Roxie moved to Austin, Texas, promising it would only be temporary, but had the opportunity to be in a big-time off-Broadway show, and Blake traveled up north to Vancouver for a really cool paid internship at her favorite fashion house. Something told me she would be less likely to move back. Watching them move on to bigger and better things made me wish I could just pack up and move, too, but I always felt like I was being kept in the Portland area for something or someone. When we moved here after leaving home, I could never understand why my parents chose Beaverton. All they would ever say was, "Someday, you'll understand." It wasn't that I didn't like it, and the thought of not having my best friends was tortuous, but they could have chosen anywhere once we made that choice to transition. I was grateful we chose to leave the Parallel and come to Earth because I knew since day one it's where I wanted to be, but Beaverton, Oregon, seemed like an odd destination to choose. And still, almost halfway through my 20s, I didn't have my promised "why."

What did they mean by someday?

How much older do I need to be?

Perhaps the "why" was to meet my friends. There hadn't been much else that made sense but my best friends.

Roxie, Blake, and I had already planned our first visit since they moved. I was dying a little without them in my daily life, so a visit seemed appropriate. We decided we would all meet where Blake was, since neither fRoxie or I had ever been to Canada. We vowed to make this trip annual at the very least, but I knew upfront that annual would not be enough.

How am I supposed to live without them here?

I missed them terribly, but thankfully, that is where my coworkers stepped in. Obviously, no one in the world could replace Roxie and Blake, but I had to find a way to function without them, and I needed a social life, despite having no time to think outside of work, even if it meant having friends at my apartment to binge-watch "Intervention" and drink coffee. I needed to have some remnants of a social life.

Coffee breaks and lunchtime at work quickly became some of my favorite times. I could make my daily phone calls to the girls, check on my parents, and get to know my coworkers a little better. The conversations weren't always great, but I made sure Dr Pepper was on hand to help me get through those. The best time of the day, however, was clocking out. Decompressing was key in this career, and for that reason, I always have a pair of running shoes on me, and a permanent supply of Ruzzo and Dr Pepper in my fridge.

Being a nurse was hard, harder than I ever expected, and maybe the department I was in exacerbated the rough patches, but I never imagined the rough patches to feel like sandpaper on my soul. And yet, experiencing all that in my first couple of years of nursing still didn't take away my joy of providing comfort and solace to people in some of their lowest and most desperate times. Learning their stories was welcomed, joyous, and incredibly sad. Some were full of the wildest chapters. You could tell when they shared them that they got to experience all of the memories again, and it gave them life. Then there were the ones who barely made it out of the dedication pages, and those were the ones that required a full day of recovery, sometimes two. Those were the ones that made me question how any person could choose such a profession or how faith continued to show its presence. Watching a child suffer made me question life on multiple occasions, and yet you could sit with these kids and learn more from them in two weeks than six years of college. Time and time again, I was blown away by their wisdom.

Although I adored many of my patients, it was the ones on the two ends of the spectrum of life that really got my wheels turning.

Would I get to be one of them?

Would I get to have one of them?

Does where I come from complicate matters?

Note to self: I need to ask Mom and Dad about that.

I had so many thoughts and questions, and so I soaked in all of the information I could—the love, loss, and tragic happiness that came in between. It was clear that the patients I encountered would become much more than a full name, date of birth, and a scan of a hospital wrist band.

Little did I know how much.

Chapter Twelve
(Essi)

"Lorna, you know you can't leave here until you eat something. It's the same every week," I playfully chastised her.

"And?" she snapped back the way she always had.

"And I will sit here and annoyingly ask you all sorts of life questions until your irritation outweighs your hunger and you eat. Don't do that to us. Don't make us annoyed at each other," I giggled, "Eat. Please."

Lorna called my bluff really quick and said, "EmJ, you should know by now that telling stories is possibly my favorite pastime. If you are trying to blackmail me into eating, I will outlast you here.

If you want me to eat, you are gonna have to sit and eat with me while you endure one of my stories."

Good God, you are stubborn.

It was always a struggle to get Lorna to eat. She was in her early 60s, a widow, and had a grown kid, and all the time in the world. Each week for the first few months, she thought she manipulated me into sitting and eating my lunch with her, but over time, it was the only place I wanted to eat my lunch.

Anyone on the chemotherapy and infusions floor will tell you that almost nothing sounds good when you feel that nauseated, but she would ask me to eat with her as if somehow watching me eat allowed her to enjoy the food vicariously through me.

Lorna quickly became one of my favorite patients, one of my favorite people, really. Although I hated that she was a regular, I loved that she scheduled her treatments only on days I was working, and I loved providing her with the company she was clearly missing.

There was something so familiar about her, so comforting, and I took to her fast.

Who is comforting who here?

She had the kindest face, an incredibly soft voice, and the gentlest demeanor. It was such an odd feeling and extremely hard to explain, even to myself, but she made me feel like home. She made me feel like I could legitimately sit with her for hours, and yet until she walked through those hospital doors, I had never known her a day in my life.

That is what I loved though, about being a nurse—the connections.

Lorna was a different kind of connection, though. I genuinely loved her. Ironically and a bit sadistic, I looked forward to her treatments every week. Of course, I would have also been overjoyed to watch her ring that bell, but I knew that wouldn't come without a sense of abandonment on my end. The irony was not lost on me. I knew Lorna felt the same connection because she told me on more than one occasion, and it was so validating to have those feelings reciprocated.

It took her a while to open up to me, but once she did, it was as if a dam had broken, and all her stories flooded in. I got to hear amazing stories of her late husband and her son. And although she never went into detail about their personal information, I never thought to ask. Her stories were so vivid that I felt like I knew them, even though she never told me their names.

It was clear she loved and missed her husband very much. The topic of remarrying came up at some point in our many conversations, and Lorna was adamant that it would never happen.

"Truth be told, it has never crossed my mind," she said.

"What? Really?" I asked, a bit shocked.

"Really. We shared such a significant love that anything else would be the universe's sad attempt at a joke. It wouldn't be fair to whoever else I gave a chance. The bar was set so high, he made it unreachable for other people. A blessing and a curse I guess you could say," she laughed. "He gave me enough love in 25 years to last the rest of my life."

I sat there in silence to digest what she said.

I had so many questions that quickly blossomed into concern, and somehow, she could read it on my face.

"What's wrong, EmJ?" Her inquiry was gentle.

"No, nothing is wrong. I mean, I love your story, but I think you are one of the lucky ones. I just… I don't think that exists anymore. Like I don't think I will ever find that kind of love," I replied in sadness.

"Oh, trust me, honey. You will," she reassured me. "Yes, I know I was one of the lucky ones, and I am grateful every day for the love he gave me, but I genuinely believe we all have our soulmates. Sometimes you have to be willing to come out of the shadows to be found. I try to tell my son that all the time, but he has this outrageous idea, and has since he was a kid, that his soulmate is his childhood best friend." She waved her hand dismissively, shook her head, and exhaled. "It's a long story and you wouldn't believe it if I told you. I barely believe it to be honest."

Now I'm intrigued.

"What do you mean? Tell me more," I requested.

She just stared at me and gave a half-grin.

It was a small smile in an attempt to hide her sadness, but I couldn't piece together why.

"Oh, come on, you have to tell me now. I'm invested! It's not like I will ever meet him, and if I do, I promise I won't embarrass him!" I begged.

"Weirder things have happened with my son," she sighed. "As a mom, I would be lucky to have my son want to meet you."

"Don't get any ideas," I laughed. "I'm still hiding in the shadows, remember?"

"Well, it wouldn't matter if you were. He has made it clear his heart is spoken for. She's a mystery, but maybe someday she will come back to him," she exhaled.

It seemed like an odd direction for our conversation to go but I could tell it was depressing her, and that was the exact opposite of my intentions, so I quickly changed the subject.

I reached for her lunch box to help set out her lunch. That was one of the things she had told me her husband used to do, and she really missed it. Sometimes, in this profession, redirection was key.

I set her sandwich out first, unwrapped her carrots, and opened her Dr Pepper.

Smart lady. Another thing we have in common.

I accidentally dropped her bag with her napkin, so I quickly bent down to grab it.

"I'm sorry. I'm so clumsy. Let me grab that for you," I said.

As I reached over her to pick it up, my necklace slid out from underneath the collar of my shirt. I had only just started wearing this particular necklace since finding it at my parents' house a few weeks ago. I had never seen it before, but as I was scrounging through my dad's drawer for laundry quarters, it sort of came out from hiding underneath his change tray.

Yes, I still go to my parents' house for laundry money.

I didn't understand the meaning of its inscription, and my dad was as vague about that as he was about our moving location, but he let me have it without putting up a fight. My mom just smiled when I showed it to them. I saw her squeeze Dad's hand as if to pass all of her excitement on to him.

Odd.

"We'll explain it to you someday, but you can take it," he said coyly.

Ugh. Again?

What does that even mean?

"You guys realize I'm not a child anymore, right? Like, I have a job, live on my own..."

"And you still come here for laundry quarters," he said before I could get another word out of my mouth.

Touché, Dad.

At times, I didn't have the energy to argue with their cryptic innuendos, so I let them be, but I was surprisingly fond of the necklace, so I kept it. In just a few short weeks, I had grown to love it and its mysteriousness. It was a small padlock. At times, it felt heavy to wear. It was as if it held emotions inside of it that bore the weight of the world.

When it slipped out of my shirt, it swung in front of Lorna's face, which turned as pale as the white scrubs I was wearing.

"Lorna?"

Oh, shit, what's happening?

I grabbed her wrist to take her pulse, but she just stared at me with her bright blue speckled eyes glued to my face.

Is she having a stroke?

"Lorna, you need to speak to me, or I am calling for help," I begged her.

She closed her eyes and re-lived something in her mind. When she opened them, she looked at me with utter confusion.

"Lorna, please, you're scaring me," I insisted. "I'm calling for help."

I stood up and ran for the phone because I was so unsure of what else to do.

"Essi?" she asked.

I froze dead in my tracks.

What did she just say?

I turned around and met her confusion with my own. She was standing up with her hand over her mouth, trying to conceal her shock.

"I have never told you my real name. How did you know that?"

Through her gasp and stutter, she finally got out the words she was grasping to find.

"It's impossible," she whispered.

She started to rip out all of her IVs and just kept repeating that she needed to leave, even though I was begging her to stay and tell me what was going on. More importantly, I wanted an answer as to how she knew my name when I hadn't given it to anyone at this hospital except for the HR department.

Before I had a chance to stop her, she was fleeing out of our department, through the lobby doors, and into the parking lot, quicker than a fugitive.

All I could do was stand there speechless, unable to process anything that had just happened.

What in the world is going on?

Chapter Thirteen
(Derek)

My mom called me, leaving a very frantic voicemail. Of course, it was the middle of the night in Iceland, so I didn't get her message until I was awake, but when I listened to it, my heart sank into quicksand.

"Derek, hi, it's Mom. Listen, I need you to call me back. Um... there's something really important I need to talk to you about. I'm fine, promise, but call me back, okay?"

I immediately started to walk to the gym to speak with my coach because I was assuming the worst.

I couldn't call her back because, of course, it was the middle of the night in Portland once I got her voicemail. So, I wanted to work fast on my end, in case what she was telling me was that I needed to be home. The team and management had always been on board if I needed to go home for her, so I made sure they knew what was going on.

"You will have a ticket in the morning if that's what you need, Derek," my coach said with the utmost certainty.

And that's exactly what happened.

My mom was the most cryptic she had ever been and refused to tell me anything that was going on, but I could tell she was freaked out.

"Hi, sweetheart. You got my voicemail?" she asked me.

"Yes, Mom, I did. What's going on? Tell me you're okay, please," I implored.

"I'm okay. I- I mean, I'm not, but I am. Listen," she sighed, "it's really hard to explain, but I need you to come home right away. This cannot wait."

"Mom, you can't ask me to leave in the middle of my season without telling me why. Seriously, what is going on?" I exclaimed. She was silent for a few more seconds.

What is she not saying?

"Mom, are you okay? Is everyone else okay?" I asked, hoping for a little more clarification. "You're being so cryptic and weird. Just tell me what's happening!"

"I am still doing treatments every week, but they're not going great," she admitted.

Fuck. I knew it.

"I feel everything I was feeling before you left. I'm just a little more tired and worn out and not making much progress. I just need you here for a little while. Is that doable?"

She was being pushy and stubborn.

"And this can't wait until I come home for Christmas in a few weeks?" I inquired.

"No, it's really important that you're here," she asserted.

Important for who?

"Okay," I agreed with hesitation. "The team said I would be able to leave in the morning, so I will get everything packed and be home in Portland tomorrow afternoon."

"Perfect. I have treatment in the early evening. You can meet me there after you land," she said, almost sounding excited.

"Uh, are you sure you'll still be there? Maybe-"

She quickly cut me off. "Oh, I will be there. Meet me there, okay?"

Geez, is it really that bad?

On my flight back to the States, I sat on the airplane, rattling my brain for all the possible scenarios happening with Mom. She said the treatments weren't working, but I didn't know if that meant her cancer was progressing or not getting better. Her secrecy was almost cruel because I put myself in knots playing out each scenario.

Am I saying goodbye to her?

No. She would have told me, right?

Although the flight from Iceland to Portland was direct and only eight hours, it felt like the longest day of my life. I was reminded quickly of the day my mom told me she had cancer, and I couldn't help but think this time might be worse.

I landed in Portland at 3:00 pm, and it was much different weather in early December than when I left in September. Although I had learned to live with the homesickness after being in Iceland for almost two seasons, it still felt amazing to touch down at home. I just wished it wasn't for these circumstances.

My first season was hard, really hard. So many times, I was ready to quit and go back home with my mom and friends. Although I got to talk with Mom often, and it made me feel like I wasn't missing much, there was a lot of guilt for not being with her while she was enduring her chemo.

I know she would have made the guilt worse had I stayed, so I guess it was the lesser of two evils, but I think there would always be a part of me that longed to be home, no matter how comfortable I was in Europe. I had no clue, though, how long playing would last, so I did my best to dive in and experience every part of it. Eventually, I came into my own on the team, and just as I thought, Aggi quickly became a close friend. I spent a lot of time with him and his wife, Svava, and he eventually taught me how to play poker, which became a Friday night event every week. Besides the game schedule, it was one of the few things I really looked forward to doing. Aggi talked so much shit about how much money he would take of mine, but I for sure have taken way more of his.

Being overseas is beyond cool, but it is also insanely lonely, so being home, despite the reason, is a fresh breath of PDX air.

As I walked off the plane and down the long hallway to reach customs, just before hitting the escalators, I was reminded I was home with one image—a huge mural of the Portland skyline, the infamous Portland Stag, and words that read "Welcome to the United States of America - Portland, Oregon."

The sight of the mural brought comfort and a sense of peace before what was sure to be a morose evening. I stared at the mural until I descended underneath it, and the only thing I could see at the bottom of the escalator was the dreaded, 45-minute-long customs line.

How can I get to the front of that?

I waited through the line, finally grabbed my luggage from baggage claim, exited customs, and was ecstatic to see the first familiar face after landing. Joshua was waiting for me with his big smile, an ice-cold Dr Pepper, and a fresh cup of Black Rock Coffee, my favs. He held them in each of his hands and stretched out his arms for a big hug.

"Hey, bud! Long time no see. Let me look at you," he said. He took a step back to give me a once over in only the fashion he could, and his face of approval gave me a slight boost in confidence.

"Dang, D, you been lifting weights," he said as he grabbed around my biceps as if to make sure they were real.

He handed me the drinks and said, "You're gonna need these."

Shit, he talked to my mom.

She told him before me?

"What do you know?" I admonished him.

"Nothing, bro. Your mom wouldn't say anything, just that she had some news, you were coming home, and I needed to pick you up and take you to the hospital to meet her. It just didn't sound like it would be a great situation with the hospital stuff, so I figured you could use these, that's all."

"But it is good to see you," he said with a grin.

"Yeah, man. It's good to see you, too. I wish it wasn't for this, but I appreciate you giving me a ride."

The context clues were starting to pile up in a negative direction, and my brain was filling in the blanks, going only one way.

As we made our way to the hospital, I looked out over the river to take in the sight of the skyline in all its glory.

It really is beautiful.

"Take my mind off of it all, man. How are things with you and Ash?" I needed to think about anything other than what I was anticipating.

Joshua beamed with excitement to answer the question.

"We're great. Better than great, in fact," he said reaching into the glove box and pulling out a small bunch of black and white pictures. "Here, take a look at these," he smiled. "I've been waiting to tell you in person."

I was handed a small set of sonogram pictures.

"What? No way! This is fucking dope, man! Congratulations!"

"It's a little out of order and all since I haven't even asked her to marry me yet, but we know we want that," he shrugged. "It just happened, but we're excited, man!"

"Josh, that's all that matters. I'm stoked for you guys! How far along is she?" I asked with genuine interest. I was intent on making sure he knew that I was genuinely happy for them, despite any bad news coming my way.

"She's about 15 weeks," he said with pride.

"I can't believe you were able to keep it from me for that long, bro!" I laughed.

It occurred to me instantly that I had not laughed in at least a few days, and it felt good.

"It was tough. Ash kept trying to get me to tell you every time we talked, but this was better."

"I appreciate that," I agreed. "This was better."

I asked him to take my mind off of everything, and he did just that. The road passed underneath us so quickly that we got to the hospital in no time at all.

"You're not coming in?" I asked him with a begging undertone.

"Shit, I mean, of course, I will if you want. I just figured this was time with you and your mom. I- I can wait here, or I can come back and get you if you need me. I'm here, no matter what she tells you, okay? Ash and I are both here for you guys."

Regardless of how much I dreaded whatever my mom was going to tell me, Josh was right. It was a moment for only Mom and me. If she was going to give me what would be tied for the worst news of my life, Josh didn't need to be there for it. He knew I would call him the moment I knew something anyway, so I took a deep breath of the brisk Portland air and closed the door.

"I'll call you. Thanks for the ride, man. It's really good to see you."

"You got it," Josh nodded, rolling up the window as his taillights exited my sight.

I could feel it. My life was about to change drastically, and I had no idea exactly how much.

Here goes nothing.

"Can you tell me how to get to the oncology ward?" I quietly asked the woman at the information desk.

My mom had yet to allow me to come to one of these appointments, and as I walked through the hospital, I was almost furious at myself for not insisting that I accompany her sooner, while I was home.

I'm here now.

My hands and head were sweating so much that it felt like I had just poured water on myself. I removed my beanie with the intent to relieve the heat exiting my body, but it was useless. The only thing that would bring any relief would be to hear my mother say she was okay. I was preparing myself for the worst and praying for the best.

They should have bars in hospitals.

"Through the purple elevators to the 4th floor... and then to your personal hell."

Stop that.

I got this. I'm ready.

"Hi. I hope I'm in the right place. I'm here to see my mom who is doing chemo today. Lorna Ivey."

"Sign in, please," she directed me. "I'll take you to her room."

As we walked down the hall, the nurse was kind and complimentary of my mom. "Your mom is the absolute sweetest. I mean, you probably already know that, but we really enjoy her around here. You're lucky." Her smile was genuine and comforting, and I quickly understood why she would be good at her job.

Is my "parent luck" running out?

Jesus, Derek, you're being so morbid.

"That's really nice of you to say, but yes, I agree. She's pretty great."

The nurse led me to her room where Mom was sitting alone in her recliner with her eyes closed and hands clenched. It was one of her nervous tells, and it immediately made my fears come more to life, but she looked serene and peaceful—a juxtaposition and a sight for sore eyes.

"Hi, Mom..."

Her eyes burst open with tears already in them and she reached for me to hug her. I could hear the catch in her throat despite desperately trying to hide it, and she just hugged me.

"Hi, babe," she finally whispered. "I'm so glad you're here."

She pulled away to get a better look at me, and without another word, cupped my right cheek the way she always has and hugged me again. I could feel her tears drop to my shirt, and my heart dropped with them.

"Mommy, it's okay." I gave her one big squeeze and asked for confirmation of my fears. "Tell me. What is it? Is it bad? Are you okay?"

She looked at me with the most genuine smile and gave me a wildly unexpected answer.

"I am more than okay. In fact, I have never been better."

What the fuck?

"What are you talking about, Mom?" I laughed out of nervousness. "Why am I here if you're okay?"

I looked at her with pure confusion. I was trying to decipher her words while reading her face and body language, and it was sending my brain in a thousand different directions.

Chemo brain is a thing, but does it cause confusion?

What is she talking about?

"Derek," she braced herself at the edge of her chair, the best she could. "I found her," she said through her unforgiving tears. "Or… or she found me, I- I don't know. I don't know how it's possible, I don't understand it at all, but she's here, honey."

My confusion was playing tug of war with my anguish and anger, and I couldn't decide how to react.

There was only one "she," only one "her," and my mom's words were starting to feel like a cruel joke, but I couldn't depict what she was suggesting. Her words and sentiment seemed genuine, but I was baffled at her implication.

I knew back then that my mom only accepted Essi because she accepted me. That she only accepted the thought of Essi because she couldn't stand the thought of pushing me further away, but deep down, I always felt that she didn't believe me. Or maybe she wanted to, but she couldn't.

"Mom," I took a deep breath, "who's here? Who did you find? Please stop being so cryptic and just tell me why I flew thousands of miles home and missed my game, if it wasn't because of your cancer." My hands were starting to speak for me.

Calm down.

"Derek," she said, grabbing my hands firmly, "she's here. Essi is here."

A blended combination of anxiety, panic, and anger started to fill my chest. I could feel the angst starting to form into words, and before I said anything I would regret, I began my retreat.

I pushed her hands away to let go of mine, walked to the corner to grab my backpack in protest, and geared up to leave.

I had never known my mom to be unkind or stupid, but this felt like both, and I needed to get out of there fast. I grabbed my phone to make the "come get me" phone call to Josh, but I turned to the sound of a knock on my mom's sliding glass door, and the reality of my mom's story punched me in the chest like a thousand bricks. The ground stripped out from underneath me, and gravity felt nonexistent. The hole in my stomach suddenly felt like the size of the hospital, and there she was, standing in the door frame with a tray of medical instruments and an IV bag.

Oh, my God.

I looked at my mom in consummate disbelief, and through her own doubt, she breathlessly said to me, "I told you it was important."

Is it her?

Is it you?

Is it really you?

I was frozen in time with a train of memories whizzing by, but the way she was frozen was different.

Her face was not showing the emotion I would have expected.

Is this like my dream?

Does she actually not remember me?

Dream was not the right word to use because it would be a fucking nightmare if the woman I had loved since the age of three had no recollection of me. My life would begin and end on the same day for the second time in my life if her memories of me were gone.

How could that be possible?

Wait, what am I saying?

How is any of this possible?

My eyes and brain were looking for any sign to convince me otherwise, and instantly, my attention was grabbed by the engraved padlock, sitting just above her breasts.

She kept her promise.

She's still wearing it.

Breathe.

There it was—the necklace I had made for her.

I grabbed for the key underneath my shirt and pulled it out to show her. I needed her to understand we were connected.

I promise you know me.

Why aren't you saying anything?

You love me.

Or loved me.

Ugh. Fuck.

I couldn't take it anymore. I needed her to hear my voice. Maybe it would alter things, and saying her name made it real for me, too.

I shook my head in disbelief as I muttered her name, and tears began to swell. "Essi?"

And her tray crashed to the floor.

It's really her.

Chapter Fourteen
(Essi)

It was one of the weirder interactions I ever had with a patient or anyone for the matter. Lorna went from someone I felt like I knew so much about to a complete mystery with one word.

Essi.

I could not wrap my head around the fact that she knew my name.

I know I'm not the only Essi in the world, but I most certainly had never met another one. Was it possible that she knew another, Essi? Yes, but what was the likelihood that she would guess my name after seeing a necklace I never knew existed before a couple of weeks ago? Near zero.

No, absolute zero.

There was too much unexplainable coincidence for it to be anything but the opposite of that.

I was worried because after Lorna ran out, I thought I might never get an explanation for the circumstances surrounding my name and how it was important to her. So, I was relieved when I saw her name and appointment back on the schedule for my next shift.

Okay, that's good. She hasn't been scared off just yet.

But wait. Why would she be scared? Shouldn't I be the nervous one?

I had so many questions I wanted to ask her. I knew I needed to be professional, but I was going to get some answers one way or another.

I called my parents to explain what happened, and not only did they not seem worried, but they almost seemed happy. I swear in the background I heard my mom say, "It's happening," but when I asked her what that meant, she clarified that what she had said was, "What's happening?"

I know what I heard. Liar.

"You're not the only Essi in the world, honey," my dad said. His implication was insulting. "You probably told her your name, and you just don't remember. Or, I mean, you work in a stressful job, Ess. Is it possible you shared it with someone else and she overheard?" His inquisition made me question the circumstances, but I could not think of a time when I gave that information to anyone, so the answer was no.

"You guys are acting so weird. Why are you not more weirded out by this?" I asked.

"Essi, why would we be? You have told us for months about your favorite patient, Lorna. Who cares if she knows your real name?"

"No, Dad, that's not it. It's not only that she knew my name. It was like she knew me! It was as if she recognized the necklace. Like, how is that possible?"

"Maybe she does know you. Be patient." He laughed hard at his dad joke and was obviously trying to deflect and steer the conversation elsewhere. "Pardon the pun," he said, and I could hear his grin through the phone.

Whatever.

I rolled my eyes, huffed as loud as I could, and said goodbye. It was clear that my conversation with them was not going the way I expected, and ultimately, he was right. I was going to have to wait until I saw Lorna again to shed my uneasiness.

When I sat and really tried to think through my interactions with Lorna, I couldn't come up with any indication before seeing the necklace when she acted like she knew me.

What does this charm have to do with all of this?

The mysteriousness of my necklace was starting to cause more alarm than wonder. I was wracking my brain to come up with alternative stories, but there weren't any, I was sure of it.

My shift could not get here fast enough. I knew once I got to the hospital that Lorna would have already been there for 45 minutes or so, and that made me feel like I was on the wrong end. I tried to get Erin, one of the morning nurses, to switch shifts with me, so I could be there first, but she couldn't accommodate, so not only did I have to be there after Lorna's appointment started, but I also had to sit and wait in my desperation for my shift to start. "The Waiting Place" was as bad as Dr. Suess warned.

I tried everything to mask my apprehension. I went to the gym and tried to sweat it out. I went to Target to see if some retail therapy could help but to no avail. Lunch at my favorite restaurant and brewery did wonders for my soul, and although one could argue that the food at Cooper Mountain Ale Works was indeed magic, it did not speed up the time like I wanted.

I watched the clock in hopes it would somehow make the hands go faster, but it felt as if time slowed down instead. I couldn't remember the exact day I felt this anxious, but I know there was one. I felt like the new girl on my first day of school many years ago. And just like the 16-year-old new girl, I only need two things right now to help—Roxie and Blake.

I don't know how I didn't think to call them sooner, but they would surely have better advice than my parents. I texted them in our group text: *I need to talk to you guys ASAP. Can we have an ER facetime session in five?*

Within 30 seconds, I had a text back from each of them.

Roxie: *Duh.*

Blake: *I'll take my break early. Call you in four.*

"Oh, my God, I have missed your fucking faces," Roxie said. "We shouldn't go this long not talking again."

"We talked like three days ago," Blake interjected.

"Whatever, it's too long." Roxie snapped back. "Okay, but enough of that. Es, what's up? Are you good?"

"Yeah, sorry for the 9-1-1, I just need your ears about something," I said to them.

"Okay, we're here. Shoot," Blake said calmly.

I gave them the rundown of the last couple of days. I talked to them just about every other day, so Lorna was already a familiar name to them, but they also knew I went by the nickname they gave me and that no one at the hospital knew me by Essi. So, it was weird to them how the conversation with Lorna ended. Blake and Roxie's faces showed all the confusion as mine the day it happened.

"She called you Essi, and then just ran out? And you think it's because of the necklace?" Roxie asked, perplexed. "Dude, have we seen this whimsical piece of jewelry yet?" I paused to showcase the padlock charm, and neither of them seemed overly impressed. "Yeah, that is super strange, Roxie said, "I'm so confused."

"Right!? I'm freaking out about it. Like, how does she know me?"

"What is Lorna's last name," Blake asked. "Let's look her up on soc meeds and make sure she's not some creepy stalker."

"No, I can't do that," I rejected the idea.

"Well, maybe you can't, but I can," she said sarcastically.

"No, Blake. I can't give out her personal info. I probably shouldn't have even told you her first name."

"But you did, and now your BFFs want to make sure you're safe," she raised her voice.

"I'm safe, silly," I assured them, "but I just needed you guys to hear the story and agree with me that it was weird. It's weird, right?"

They both echoed my feelings about the whole thing, which somehow gave me a sense of relief. I got a play-by-play of their weekends and their single-life shenanigans, and by the time we hung up, I hadn't realized the clock hands had made their move, and I was going to be late for my shift.

Dummy.

I scrambled to get ready to go, and with the time dwindling faster than it had all day, I didn't have time to put on makeup or fix my hair into anything other than a big messy bun.

I gave myself a once over in the mirror, let out a big sigh, and rolled my eyes at my reflection, as I walked out the door.

Who am I kidding?

This is how I leave the house every day.

Why would today be any different?

After sitting in a little of that lovely Rose City traffic, I finally got to the hospital and clocked in. Joelle was in the office as I walked in, and she interrupted her conversation with one of the other nurses to address me. "EmJ, I heard something strange happened with Lorna the other day, something I need to know about on your end?"

Shit. Why? Am I in trouble?

"No, I don't think so. She's here today for her infusion so I was going to talk to her and make sure everything was okay."

She nodded. "Alright. Well, let me know if you need me for anything. Yeah?"

"Yeah," I obliged.

Whew. Dodged a Joelle bullet. No one likes those.

I got my tray ready for my rounds, which included Lorna's second bag of IV. I had other patients to tend to, but I was only interested in seeing her and knowing how this chapter would end. I checked in on my other patients as quickly as I could, so I had the chance to spend more time hearing Lorna's explanation if she would even give one to me. At that point, I wasn't sure she wanted to talk to me, but I was going to be as professional as possible and still try.

I finished with my last check-in before heading to her room. Her curtains were closed behind the glass doors, which wasn't her normal forte, but as I got closer to her room, I could see someone else was in there with her. She never had visitors, so I was more than frustrated that my story might have to wait until another day.

I approached the door to knock and could hear a muffled conversation. I was weary to encroach on their privacy, but it was something, as a nurse, that I did all the time. I wasn't sure why this time was different.

I quietly knocked, slid open the sliding glass door, and pulled back the curtain to peek in the room. Lorna was talking to what I could only imagine was her son. Her face was red and damp from crying, and I immediately felt a need to step in and protect her. I couldn't see who she was talking to because as I pulled back the curtains, he had his back to me and was picking up his bag, looking like he was getting ready to leave.

Good. Bye. I need to talk to your mom.

Lorna looked at me and smiled as if nothing had happened the other day. I saw her shoulders relax, and tears began to fall from her eyes again. The man in her room turned his head in attention to my presence in the doorway. He stood up stiffly and dropped both his bag and his jaw to the floor, and he looked at Lorna with an expression of disbelief.

I was in a bit of my own as I recognized him as the man that I had fantasized about since watching him play basketball a couple of years ago.

Why is Derek Ivey in this fucking room right now?

Omg, Essi, you idiot. Lorna Ivey. How did you not put the names together by now? It's her son.

My God, he's beautiful.

My heart was beating so fast, but I was frozen. I wanted to speak but I couldn't get my mouth to move or my tongue to create words. I watched Lorna muffle through her tears. "I told you it was important."

What? What was important?

Me? This?

Will someone tell me what the fuck is happening?

I couldn't move or speak. I couldn't look away from the movie playing out in front of me or understand why I was in it. Derek was fumbling with something under his collar and pulled out a small key from around his neck as if to show me as evidence.

I looked down and examined my padlock charm.

They match.

What in the hell does this mean?

I don't understand.

And then he said one word, and my entire life flashed before my eyes.

"Essi?" he whispered, astonished.

Oh, my God.

I could feel the tray leave my grasp as my fingertips lost their grip, and there was nothing I could do to stop it from crashing to the floor.

Tears welled in my eyes as my memory came to life and filled in blanks that hadn't made sense for almost a decade. It was as if Derek saying my name unlocked everything and removed a veil that had been hiding him all this time.

My brain quickly took me through a time-warp of our lives growing up, and I remembered everything—our games, his dad, our fights, the dance, the red dress, and the last time we saw each other where he told me he loved me.

Instantaneously, I understood Lorna's reaction after she saw my necklace and why my parents' reaction was borderline happy with my story. I understood why I felt such a connection to a complete stranger that day at PSU, and how watching him look at Barbie almost broke me. I understood all the cryptic conversations with my parents.

Beaverton finally makes sense.

Although I was sure there were some rules broken moving here, I was going to hug the shit out of my parents the next time I saw them because it was clear they did this for me. My dreams of him connected so easily now. My mind had been trying its damnedest to give him back to me. All this time, he was right here, and I never knew. The man in front of me wasn't my fantasy. He was the missing piece, the reason no relationship until now could keep my attention or work. The reason I always knew in the deepest parts of my soul there was more. My feelings for this man were born from my adoration of a three-year-old little boy and grew over 13 years to become all-consuming. What I'm feeling again is the love I have dreamt of, the love that makes all others seem novice—an unparalleled love. The man standing in front of me was my best friend and the absolute love of my life.

Although it felt like hours, only seconds had passed into my revelation, but I could feel Derek's trepidation. His eyes were full of worry and wonder, and he looked like he was waiting for or anticipating my rejection.

You're torturing him.

I couldn't make him wait any longer.

I nodded in acknowledgment, and with the biggest smile I could muster through my tears, I answered back to him, "It's me."

Derek burst into tears, and I ran to him.

I leaped into his arms, and we hugged each other for the first time in nine years, two months, and 12 days.

I bawled in his shoulder and neck, and it felt as perfect a fit for my face as it had the last time I saw him and cried there.

I looked at Lorna, who was on the edge of her seat as if she was watching the happy ending to a great romantic comedy movie. I mouthed to her "thank you," and I could see all over her face the only thank you she needed was happening right in front of her.

I pulled away to look up at him in bewilderment, and with tears still streaming down my face, and whispered, "You found me."

He gently cupped my chin in his fingertips, wiped my tears away, and through his own, he chuckled, "Technically, it was my mom who found you. Can you believe that?"

We both laughed.

The irony was profound, and not lost on either of us.

He continued, "I felt you. I never gave up that you'd come back to me. I knew we'd find each other again."

"I have missed you every day."

I couldn't catch my breath or compose myself to say anything else, but I knew I wanted only one thing at that moment, and it was to feel his lips on mine.

My eyes and hands said everything I wanted to say, and it was clear he felt the same. Without his eyes ever leaving mine he asked, "Essi Michelle Jackson, can I kiss you?"

You better.

I exhaled, "The answer is yes, forever."

Epilogue

I got home from school to a look of utter angst from my parents.

Oh, no. I know that look and it's not good.

My mom walked to meet me at the door, handed me a piece of paper, and said, "Go there. You need to hurry."

With complete confusion, I opened the torn, folded piece of paper and didn't recognize the address she had scribbled onto it. It was a Portland address, but I had never been there.

"Essi, you need to go now if you're going to make it," my dad said sternly.

Make it?

"Make what? What is it, you guys? What aren't you telling me?" I pleaded with them. "Is it Derek?" I asked as I silently prayed it wasn't.

"No, sweetheart, it's not Derek. But just trust us, you need to go."

With hesitation and worry, I shuffled my feet back out of the door I had just walked in but with a completely different demeanor.

Where are they sending me?

I couldn't help but feel a huge hole in my stomach. Something bad was happening, but Mom and Dad would not have sent back through at that moment unless it was important. I found the street sign associated with the address and went right there.

Oh, no, what am I seeing?

Right there in the middle of the intersection was a mangled Silver SUV that looked as if it had gotten into a fight with a train. The maroon sedan that it was intertwined with didn't look much better, and there was no indication that the people in either of the cars were okay. The SUV had been crushed from the front bumper into the passenger side seat, and there was a lot of chaos happening in front of me.

I could hear cries and screams, and the police and ambulance sirens were echoing in the distance on their way to a horrific scene.

I started to walk towards the crash, and then it hit me why my parents sent me there.

Derek's dad drives a silver SUV.

My walk instantly became a run, and as I reached the car, I was met with the exact situation I was dreading. It was Derek's dad, John, or Johnny as Lorna fondly called him.

No, no, no, no, no, no, no.

He was still in the driver's seat of his car, seatbelt still on, holding his left arm and chest, wincing in pain. I couldn't be sure of what his injuries were but there was a lot of commotion and he looked pale, trying to take hundreds of small shallow breaths.

Oh, no! Just hang on. They're coming.

He had his eyes open, observing the scene unfolding in front of him. People were starting to get out of their cars and attempt to provide aid where they could. A couple of people rushed to his car, ignoring me of course, and John was more concerned with the child in the other car, pleading that they tend to the family first. He was assuring the bystanders that he was okay, so they would focus their attention on them.

Not now! Don't be selfless now.

"He's lying! Help him!" I was screaming, but obviously no one could hear me. Derek's dad was dying in front of me, and I couldn't help him.

What do I do? I have to try something.

On a whim, I made a choice and hoped and prayed I wouldn't be punished for it.

For only the second time in my life, I was visible to another human.

"Mr. Ivey, just hang on, okay? They're coming. Can you hear the sirens? They're coming to help. You gotta hang on. Derek needs you." The tears were starting to drop because I could feel that time was dwindling.

I was fumbling in the car, trying to unbuckle him to see where he was hurt, and he grabbed my hand.

"Essi?"

His question shocked me, and I turned to meet his very pale face with a small smile. I nodded.

"It must be pretty bad if I can see you," he said with some of his standard sarcasm.

"No, I just—" I couldn't get any more words out before he interrupted me.

"It's okay, honey. Someday, not today, because he won't understand, tell him I'm sorry. Tell him I love him more than anything in all the universes. Lorna, too."

"No, Mr. Ivey, you're gonna tell them," I tried to reassure him, even though I knew my promise was as shallow as his breathing.

"I am so glad he has you," he patted my hand, "but make sure he takes care of his mom, too. Okay?"

He was closing his eyes as the EMTs pulled up.

"Yes," I nodded and promised through my tears.

"This is not how I envisioned meeting my future daughter-in-law," he said, trying to laugh but wincing instead.

Huh? Ew.

"It's an honor and a relief to finally meet you, Essi. I hope she gets to meet you someday, too," he said, gently smiling and squeezing my hand.

I hope so, too.

He took one more deep breath, met my eyes with gratitude, and said, "Thank you, Essi," as he exhaled and closed his eyes.

The strength of his grip loosened around my fingers.

My heart sank, and just like that, Derek's dad was gone.

Made in the USA
Las Vegas, NV
04 December 2022